A Captivating Camera

"Looks almost perfect," Prue called from beneath the velvet drape of the antique camera. "Now, Phoebe, if you'll just unpeel yourself from Nikos and Piper, I'll take the first shot."

"Who died and made her Annie Leibovitz?" Piper muttered through her gritted teeth while Phoebe stifled a snort of laughter.

"Okay, looking good. Everybody ready?" Prue announced, holding her antique flashbulb aloft. "Here we go. One . . . two . . . three!"

Psfffftttt!

Piper saw the flash go off and then, for a moment, she was utterly blinded. When the bright light subsided, she squinted painfully. Then she looked down and gasped. Nikos had slithered out of her embrace and collapsed onto the floor at her feet.

"Prue. . . ." Piper started to say. She looked around her. Nikos, Chloe . . . all the pretty young things had slumped over in heaps.

More titles in the

Charmed™

Pocket Books series

THE POWER OF THREE
KISS OF DARKNESS
THE CRIMSON SPELL
WHISPERS FROM THE PAST
VOODOO MOON
HAUNTED BY DESIRE
GYPSY ENCHANTMENT
LEGACY OF MERLIN

All Pocket Books are available by post from:
Simon & Schuster Cash Sales. PO Box 29
Douglas, Isle of Man IM99 1BQ
Credit cards accepted.
Please telephone 01624 836000
fax 01624 670923, Internet
http://www.bookpost.co.uk or email:
bookshop@enterprise.net for details

SOUL OF THE BRIDE

An original Novel by Elizabeth Lenhard
Based on the hit TV series
Created by Constance M. Burge

POCKET
BOOKS

An *original* Publication of POCKET BOOKS

An imprint of Simon & Schuster UK Ltd. A Viacom Company
Africa House, 64-78 Kingsway, London WC2B 6AH

A CIP catalogue record for this book is available from the British Library

ISBN 07434 09337

5 7 9 10 8 6

Printed in Great Britain by Bookmarque Ltd, Croydon, Surrey

SOUL OF THE BRIDE

CHAPTER
1

Prue? Can I see you in my office, please?"

Prue Halliwell glanced up from the contact sheet she was inspecting to see her editor-in-chief, Nick Caldwell, waving at her from his office door. She gulped. As a photographer for *415* magazine, San Francisco's most stylish city mag, Prue was used to dealing with editors—her photo editor, the fashion editor, the restaurant critic who had her do food shots. But she hardly ever spoke to Mr. Caldwell. He was the head honcho and so out of her league, she rarely had a reason to exchange more than polite hellos with him.

Prue slipped her contact sheet into a folder and nodded at her boss, who looked, as usual, slick and polished with his graying temples and designer suit.

"Sure, Mr. Caldwell," she called. She made her way across *415*'s loft, a totally hip, urban space with exposed duct work and red cement floors. Prue loved the magazine's gritty offices. And she loved her job as a *415* staff photographer—it was the most satisfying and exciting work she'd ever done. And now the big cheese was calling her into his office. Was she about to be pink-slipped?

Prue shook the horrible thought away and ran her fingers through her glossy black hair. As she approached his office door, she gave Mr. Caldwell a bright, false smile.

"What can I do for you, Mr. Caldwell?" she asked nervously.

"Come in, Prue," her editor said, taking a seat behind his desk. "And shut the door, if you don't mind."

Uh-oh, Prue thought. This does *not* look good.

"Prue," Mr. Caldwell began. "I have to tell you . . ."

Oh, Prue moaned inwardly, what good is being a witch if I can't use my powers to worm my way out of moments like this one?

". . . I love your work."

"What?" Prue blurted, her blue eyes widening. She was so ready for a layoff, she couldn't quite believe her ears.

"Your photographs are really vibrant," Mr. Caldwell said. "You clearly have a lot of talent, even if it is still a little raw."

"Thank you!" Prue replied. She could feel herself flushing with happiness. Who needs magic, she thought giddily, when I have . . . talent!

"Here's the deal," Mr. Caldwell said. "We have nothing planned for the August cover. I want to give you a chance. If, and *only* if, you shoot a picture that knocks my socks off, the cover's yours."

"A-and . . . the topic?" Prue stuttered.

"That's up to you, Prue," Mr. Caldwell responded with a sly smile. "Could be a big break for you. But know that other photographers are going to be trying for the cover, too. You've got some healthy competition, so do your best."

"Of course," Prue said, standing up.

Clearly, Mr. Caldwell didn't know her too well. Were they here, her younger sisters, Piper and Phoebe, would have been happy to tell him, Prue Halliwell always does her best. She was a perfectionist with a capital *P*—a classic eldest child. "Thank you for the opportunity, sir. I promise to knock your socks off."

With a grin, Prue turned and headed out of the office. In fact, she headed straight out of 415. She was too exhilarated to pore over contact sheets. She had to come up with a killer cover idea. She needed to go home, where she could think and maybe bounce some ideas off her sisters.

Ever since Prue, Piper, and Phoebe had moved into their grandmother's big San Francisco mansion, they'd relied on one another for just about everything—professional and romantic advice, party clothes, and oh yeah, their magical powers.

They had discovered that they were witches—the Charmed Ones—when Phoebe found *The Book of Shadows* in the attic. The enormous, ancient tome was filled with incantations, potions, and information passed down by generations of Halliwell witches, including their grandmother and mother. Mom and

Grams were both gone now, leaving only Prue and her sisters to carry on their Charmed legacy.

The freakiest thing was, they were the most powerful witches of all. Individually, each sister packed a wallop. But when they worked together, they had the Power of Three. It made them almost unbeatable. Not that a host of demons and evil warlocks didn't routinely try to conquer them, anyway.

Yup, Prue thought sarcastically as she unlocked the door of her BMW, good things always happen in threes, don't they?

The thing about their new lives as witches was, sometimes their gifts could be a big pain in the butt.

"I mean," Prue muttered as she steered her Beamer toward home, "how do I explain to a date that I can telekinetically toss things out the window with a flick of my finger? Or that Piper can freeze time and Phoebe has premonitions about the future, *plus* she can fly." Phoebe's ability to go airborne was a recent development, and it was a power she *totally* hadn't mastered yet.

I can just see it now, Prue imagined with a dry laugh. My date's giving me a good-night kiss on the front porch and I have to say, Oh, that witch flying by on the vacuum cleaner? Don't mind her. She's just my little sister.

The sisters' mandate, that they protect the innocent, could be inconvenient, too, Prue thought irritably. Saving the world was always getting in the way of her work.

"But not this time," she murmured with determination. "*Nothing's* going to come between me and this cover. Nothing!"

*   *   *

Nothing makes me happier than being in an art class, Phoebe Halliwell thought as she strode to the sink to rinse out her paintbrushes. She looked over her shoulder at the classroom. It was milling with other art students who were wrapping up their projects as well. Phoebe's work in progress was over by the window—right next to the diminutive, flame-haired Professor Winters.

In fact, Phoebe realized with a gulp, the professor—her art adviser *and* her harshest critic—was scrutinizing Phoebe's canvas at that very moment. Ho boy, Phoebe thought. She put down her brushes and hurried over.

"I was trying for a little O'Keeffe and a little van Gogh," Phoebe announced as she stole up behind the professor.

"Yes, I see," Professor Winters said, eyeing Phoebe's abstract irises. "A bit derivative, Halliwell. Good form, but you *could* try to come up with something more original."

With that, the professor stalked away. Opened-mouthed, Phoebe stared after her.

Derivative! she thought with a disappointed frown. I thought I was inspired. I thought I was giving O'Keeffe's influence a crazy, new twist. But obviously, I thought wrong.

"Rack up another academic failure for Phoebe," she grumbled to herself, sighing deeply. School had never been her strong point, but since returning to college recently she'd been trying not to be the old, flaky, satisfied-with-a-C Phoebe.

Clearly, I haven't been trying hard enough, she

thought. She was working herself into a major funk when a low, sexy voice drifted into her ear.

"Don't listen to her. Your work's amazing."

Phoebe spun around and literally had to stop herself from gasping. Standing before her was a black-haired, paint-smeared hottie in tattered Levi's and a rainbow-daubed denim shirt. Where had *he* come from? Phoebe wondered.

As if he'd read her mind, the guy stuck out his hand.

"It's my first day in class," he said, smiling handsomely. "I'm Nikos. And *you* are clearly the star student in Painting 201. Your irises are incredible, Miss. . . ."

"Phoebe," Phoebe blurted, staring at Nikos's beautiful blue eyes. "I mean, um, Halliwell. I mean Phoebe Halliwell. But you can just call me—"

"Phoebe?" Nikos said with a teasing smile.

Phoebe would have slapped her forehead, but she had purple paint all over her palm. Instead, she merely cringed. All it takes is one gorgeous guy to reduce me to an inarticulate dork, she thought. Must deflect . . .

"So," she said, "Nikos. What kind of name is that?"

"Greek," Nikos said with a rakish grin. "I come from a huge Greek family. We go waaay back."

Opa! Phoebe thought to herself with a mischievous smile. Then she nodded at the paintbrush in the hottie's hand.

"And what are you working on . . . Nikos?"

She sidled up to Nikos's canvas and had to restrain another gasp. This may be this guy's first day in class, she thought, but he's no beginner.

"It's . . . it's hypnotizing," she whispered, gazing at the swirls of gray and brown in the damp, swampy forest scene Nikos had painted. When she squinted she could see a ghostly mansion through the trees. Wispy wraiths lurked in the shadows.

Phoebe couldn't stop staring at the painting. It seemed to go on and on, pulling her in.

"It's so dark," she breathed. Then she caught herself and glanced at Nikos.

"In a good way, I mean," she said quickly.

"Don't worry," he said with a wink. "All my deep, dark stuff is in my paintings. In real life I'm an utter optimist."

"Oh, really?" Phoebe flirted.

"Let me prove it," Nikos said. "Coffee?"

"I just happen to have the next hour free," Phoebe replied. Her heart was zinging with excitement. Now there's *really* nothing that makes me happier than being in art class, she thought. Then she shot Nikos her most sparkling smile.

"Let me just wash this purple off my hands," she said with a laugh, "and we can get outta here."

Piper was sitting at the kitchen table, one of her favorite spots in the rambling, knickknack-filled Halliwell Manor. But the sunny space was no comfort to her this afternoon, because she was doing her most dreaded task—the monthly accounting for her nightclub, P3.

She punched listlessly at her calculator. Then she turned to stare out the stained-glass window. With a sigh, she realized she was totally bored. All she did was work.

By night she played mom and manager to P3's employees. By day all her free time seemed to be spent saving innocents and fending off the constant stream of warlocks and demons intent on stealing the Halliwells' powers.

You know, Piper realized suddenly, even my power is kinda boring. Naturally I can freeze time. After all, I'm totally stagnating! Here Prue has a new, exciting career as a photographer, and Phoebe is psyched to be a college student again. Plus, my sisters are both major man magnets.

Piper cringed and thought guiltily about Leo, her White Lighter amour. Of course she adored Leo, but, well, it wasn't exactly normal to be involved with an eighty-something heavenly being. And a really busy one at that—Leo was *never* around lately. Meanwhile, real guys, mortal guys never seemed to give her a glance. She was just Piper in the middle—invisible, boring, blah.

"Hey, you'll never guess what happened to me today," called a voice, Prue's, from the front hall.

"I rest my case," Piper muttered. But then she tried to paste on a smile. It wasn't her sisters' fault that she was feeling restless and rueful.

"What happened?" she asked as Prue strode into the kitchen, tossing her purse onto the counter. She sat down at the table next to Piper, her cheeks flushed.

"Well, I—"

Slam.

That would be Phoebs, Piper thought.

"Anybody home?" the youngest Halliwell called from the front hall. "You'll never guess what happened to me today!"

Phoebe bounded into the kitchen and headed straight for the refrigerator.

"I got a fabulous opportunity at work!" Prue said, leaning forward excitedly.

"I met a fabulous guy at school!" Phoebe blurted, pulling a hunk of cheese and a fruit bowl out of the fridge.

Then both sisters started talking at once. Piper looked from Prue to Phoebe and back to Prue. This is like watching a Ping-Pong match, she thought with a giggle.

As she watched her sisters fight for airtime, Piper shook her head. The three of us could not be any more different if we tried, she thought. Prue was raven-haired and pale-skinned. She was also prompt, professional, and totally serious. Meanwhile Phoebe, who'd gone blond, had a perma-tan and a hippie's attitude, right down to her flighty career goals and forgetful nature. Piper, with her long brunette locks and beautiful bone structure, was somewhere in the middle—hard-working, a bit shy, and a total softie.

When you consider all our contrasts, Piper thought, it's amazing we're so close. But ever since they'd discovered they were the Charmed Ones, Prue, Piper, and Phoebe had been as thick as, well, a coven of witches.

Speaking of which, Piper thought, better tune in. She turned her attention back to her sisters. Somehow she managed to gather some basic information from the volley of conversation: Prue was trying out for the cover of 415, and Phoebe had met a hottie in art class. They had even had Date #1 already.

"His name is Nikos . . ." Phoebe said.

"My deadline's in ten days . . ." Prue said.

"Hey," Prue and Phoebe simultaneously blurted at each other. "Have you heard a word I just said?"

Piper burst into laughter.

"Let me fill you in," she said. While Phoebe began to chow down on some cheddar, Piper told her about Prue's big chance. Then she filled Prue in about Phoebe's new sweetie.

"Good job, Prue!" Phoebe exclaimed with her mouth full. "And I have just the model for your photo—Nikos! The guy is so hot. Slap some Calvins on him and he'll be ready to go. And, of course, you'll need an assistant, right? I volunteer! This is such a perfect way to get to know Nikos better."

Grinning with satisfaction, she took an enormous bite of an apple.

"Phoebe," Prue said with a laugh, "I don't even know what I'm going to shoot yet. Don't you think asking Nikos to model is a little premature?"

But Piper could see her little sister tuning Prue out. And if Piper knew Phoebe "I always get my man" Halliwell, she was already deep into plotting Operation Snag Nikos.

Piper couldn't resist emitting a little sigh at the thought.

"What's wrong?" Phoebe asked, slicing herself another chunk of cheese and sitting down at the table. Honestly, Piper thought, I don't know where Phoebe puts it all. She eats like a horse, and she has the figure of a fashion model.

"Nothing's wrong." Piper sighed, grabbing a piece of cheese for herself and munching on it wistfully.

"Ah, ah, ah, none of that," Prue piped up, leaning forward and peering into her sister's eyes. "Out with it. What's bugging you?"

"I just feel . . . tired, is all," Piper complained. "And, a bit mired, if you want to know the truth. Both of you have all this exciting new stuff happening in your lives. And I've just got my same old P3 books. Face it. All work and no play has made me a very dull girl."

Prue and Phoebe burst into laughter.

"Oh, thanks," Piper said sarcastically. "I can always count on my sisters to be supportive."

"I'm sorry, sweetie," Prue gasped, "but please— you're a witch with super powers, you're a total babe, you run the hottest club in town, and you're boring? I think not."

"I know what you need," Phoebe burst out. "A night on the town. How about we make a date. As soon as Prue meets her deadline, we are scheduling a sisters' night out. We'll go some place we've never been before, like that new restaurant, Heaven. I hear they have a fabulous cabaret singer. It'll be an adventure."

"Well . . ." Piper had to admit the idea of breaking out of her routine and going someplace new did cheer her up.

"It's a date," Phoebe pronounced, planting a kiss on Piper's cheek. "We will party the night away, and I will make you sorry you ever said life was boring!"

CHAPTER
2

The next morning Prue headed straight for the library. She was still racking her brain for the perfect cover idea, and she needed a little inspiration. She thought looking at some books of historic photographs might do the trick.

It's amazing, Prue thought in frustration. Photographers are always complaining about assignments and begging for an opportunity to do their own work. Now that I've been handed carte blanche, I'm paralyzed! Well, not for long.

With typical determination, Prue scoured the stacks in the photography section, choosing volume after volume—anything that might provide an idea. Finally, she staggered to a table in the reading room with a huge pile of books.

As she flipped through the first book, she spotted some black-and-white pictures of suffragettes. Hmmm, she thought. Maybe I could do a piece about powerful women in San Francisco. Prue shook her head. Nah, I want to be a little more populist. It has to be a photo everyone can relate to, especially Mr. Caldwell.

Then Prue perused some gorgeous Dorothea Lange landscapes. I love the romance of these, Prue thought, but this is so not *415*. The cover shot has to be urban.

Suddenly, a deep voice, as mellow as a fine wine, drifted over Prue's shoulder.

"I couldn't help but notice," the man said, "you've got half the photography section here."

Prue stiffened and rolled her eyes. What a lame line! You'd think she could come to the library, of all places, without having some stranger make a pass at her. She whirled around, squinting, ready to give this dude the royal brush-off.

But then something stopped her. Correction—the guy's eyes stopped her. They were gray-green with long dark lashes, and they were crinkled into the cutest smile Prue had ever seen.

"Ummm . . ." Prue said. She couldn't believe how flustered this guy was making her. Where was good ol' professional, driven Prue? Drowning in this dude's grin, that's where. Not to mention his totally athletic bod and adorable, spiky brown hair.

"I hate to disturb you, but I'm a journalist and I think you have the book I need in this enormous stack of yours," the man said.

"Oh!" Prue blurted. "I'm a photojournalist! Would you like to sit down?"

Oh my God. You don't even know this guy's name and you ask him to sit down? What are you doing, Prue? she berated herself. You have exactly nine days to get this project done, and you don't have idea one. And now you're getting chatty with some stranger?

"I'm Mitchell," the man said, straddling a chair next to Prue and thrusting out his hand. "Mitchell Pearl, *National Geographic*."

"You're kidding!" Prue said. "Working for *Geographic* is every journalist's dream. What are you researching?"

"I'm headed to Vietnam to work on a story about the new Saigon. I came here looking for a particular book of war photos," Mitchell said. Then he glanced at Prue's pile of books. "Ah, here it is! Mind if I take a look?"

"Prue Halliwell," Prue said, blushing. Blushing! Since when do I blush? she demanded of herself. "Be my guest. I was just scanning for ideas. For *415*."

"*415*, eh? Some of the city's best photographers work there," Mitchell said as he pulled the Vietnam book out of the stack. "You must be very good."

"Maybe someday," Prue said wistfully. "I'm a total rookie right now. I just got my job there this year. Now I have a shot at the cover and I can't seem to come up with the perfect idea."

"Well, you're on the right track here," Mitchell replied, pulling another book out of Prue's stack. He began flipping idly through it.

"Check out the beautiful shots in this history of Victorian portraiture, for instance," he said.

He showed Prue a sepia-tone group portrait of about nine women. They were posed formally to look like ancient Greek nobility, right down to their draped robes, biceps cuffs, and hair decorated with golden wreaths. One woman held a lyre, an ancient stringed instrument, and another was aiming a bow and arrow.

"Can I see that, Mitchell?" Prue asked, taking the book from the hottie. She read the caption beneath the photo.

" 'Victorian aristocrats embraced new camera technology by playing characters in their portraits,' " Prue read. " 'They would enact elaborate scenes. The most popular themes were classical. This group of gentleladies, for instance, were depicting the muses of ancient Greek mythology.' "

Suddenly, Prue gasped.

"That's it!" she whispered excitedly. "A feature on San Francisco's Victorian architecture. I could stage a classical tableau just like this one. And I know just where to shoot."

"See?" the gorgeous stranger said. "Was that so hard?"

"Mitchell, I have to thank you," Prue said. "I think you've just solved my dilemma. Which means, all these other books are yours for the taking. I've gotta run and get started on my idea."

Prue grabbed the book on Victorian portraiture and stood up. Mitchell jumped to his feet, as well.

"Congratulations, Prue," he said, "but don't thank me. You came up with that incredible idea all by yourself."

Prue couldn't help but smile.

"But you found just the right inspiration for me," she said. "I couldn't have done it without you."

"Well . . . if you *really* feel the need to thank me,"

Mitchell said, grinning again, "how about letting me take you to lunch tomorrow?"

"Oh, I don't know," Prue hesitated. "I've got so much work to do to make this deadline. And what about you? Aren't you jetting off to Vietnam soon?"

"Not for two weeks," Mitchell said. His smile faded. "But listen, if you're not interested, that's okay. I can take a hint."

"No!" Prue blurted. She flashed back on Piper's pity party at the kitchen table last night.

"Face it," she'd said. "All work and no play has made me a very dull girl."

Piper might as well have been talking about me, Prue thought. When I get focused on my career, I throw my personal life out the window. That's a habit I really should break.

So at that moment, she decided to throw caution to the wind. She shot Mitchell a bright smile.

"I meant to say, yes," she said. "I'd love to have lunch with you tomorrow."

"Great!" Mitchell said. His pearly whites made another brilliant appearance. "I know just the place. This Vietnamese joint just opened in the Castro and I've heard it's really authentic. If you go with me, you'll be helping me with *my* research."

"Well, I don't think you need any help, Mr. *National Geographic*," Prue teased. "But Vietnamese food sounds great."

"Pick you up at noon?" Mitchell said.

"Perfect," Prue said, slinging her purse over her shoulder. She gave him her address and headed to the circulation desk to check out her book, blushing furiously as she went.

Heading out to the parking lot a few minutes later, Prue tried to shake Mitchell's intoxicating smile out of her head. I've got to get to work, she told herself, especially if I'm going to take time out for a lunch date tomorrow.

She flopped into her Beamer and headed home. She'd been telling the truth when she'd told Mitchell she knew just where she'd shoot her portrait. In fact, she had in mind the most convenient set imaginable. After all, what more classic example of San Francisco's incredible Victorian architecture could she find than Halliwell Manor?

As Prue was leaving the library, Phoebe was just arriving home from school *and* another coffee date with Nikos. She went straight to her favorite spot in the house—the sunroom—and plopped down on one of the comfy wicker chairs. Then she stared dreamily out the window.

Nikos is perfect, Phoebe thought, sinking deeper into her chair cushion. That hour and a half at the coffeehouse just flew by. I can't believe Nikos has a thing for Georgia O'Keeffe, too. And, just like me, he's desperately searching for a career path.

"Painting's the only thing I can imagine myself doing," he'd said, flicking one of his unruly black curls out of his eyes. "And it's the only thing I'm truly good at."

"You've got that right," Phoebe had enthused, envisioning his mystical forest scene. "So what's the problem?"

"Well, you can't exactly make a living just paint-ing," Nikos had said. "At least, that's what my father keeps telling me. He's dying for me to become an accountant!"

Phoebe had closed her fingers around her throat and crossed her eyes in a dramatic mock death.

"You said it!" Nikos laughed. "I have an idea. From now on I'll paint only you. With your face, I'd make a fortune."

"Ha!" Phoebe had giggled, taking a slurp from her cappuccino.

But Nikos had stopped laughing.

"I mean it, Phoebe," he said. "You're amazing. It would be an honor to do your portrait some time."

Back in the sunroom, Phoebe closed her eyes and imagined herself lying on a green velvet chaise longue while Nikos sketched her. Move over, Kate Winslet! she thought with a giggle.

Nikos would lose himself in his canvas, drawing for an hour or more, making her look much more intriguing than she could ever look in real life. Making her . . .

"Beautiful!"

"Wha—" Phoebe's mocha-colored eyes popped open as the voice filled the sunroom. She'd been so deep in her reverie, she half expected to see Nikos standing over her. But no . . . it was only Prue, who'd clearly just walked in. She was still lugging her bulging camera bag.

"Uh, thanks, Prue," Phoebe said, raising her eyebrows. "To what do I owe the compliment?"

"Not you," Prue said bluntly.

"Hey!"

"Oh, you know you're gorgeous, Phoebe," Prue said, rolling her eyes and pulling her Nikon out of her bag. "It's just that I was looking at the sunroom. I think it'll be perfect for my *415* shoot."

Connected to the living room by a beautiful carved wood archway, the sunroom resembled a glass-enclosed birdcage. It was a white-painted sanctuary separated from their dark-and-woody living room by a pale green velvet curtain on a shiny brass rod. Usually, the sisters kept the curtain pulled back so the sunlight could spill through the house.

"You're going to shoot here?" Phoebe perked up. This was her chance to get Nikos in on Prue's shoot. It'd be a perfect way to spend more time with him.

Before Phoebe could broach the subject with Prue, Piper appeared, peeking through the sunroom entrance.

"Hello and good-bye," she said. "I'm on my way to work—back to the nightly grind at P3."

"Wait!" Prue said. "Piper, I'm going to need your help on this."

"On what?" Piper said warily, dropping her briefcase at her feet.

"My *415* shoot. I've got it all planned," Prue gushed. She pulled a thick library book out of her camera bag and showed her sisters the mythological portrait.

"I want to create a scene just like this, but with couples," she explained. "Probably four of them. They'll wear flowing robes and laurel wreaths in their hair and sandals—that whole ancient Greek thing, just the way they would have done it around the turn of the century. I'll shoot it in our sunroom. It'll be a perfect way to launch a story about San Francisco's Victorian architecture."

As she spoke, Prue lifted her camera to her eye and shot some frames of the sunroom.

"Just a few test shots," she explained. "But I think this is going to be perfect.

"That's a killer concept, Prue," Phoebe said excitedly.

"It *is* a fabulous idea," Piper agreed. "But what do you need me for?"

"Well, your classics know-how, for one," Prue said. "You're a total mythology buff. I mean, you were the only girl I knew in high school who willingly took Latin."

"Thanks, remind me of what a nerd I was," Piper said, rolling her eyes.

"Piper!" Prue protested.

"Just kidding," Piper said. "So you want a setup for four couples? That's a no brainer—the gods of Mount Olympus. You could have Zeus and Hera, and let's see, Artemis and Apollo—they were twin brother and sister gods. Then there's the world-famous Venus and Mars . . ."

"You're the goddess, Piper," Prue said, giving her sister a hug. "I knew you could set me up."

"You're welcome," Piper said, scooping up her briefcase. "Now if you'll excuse me . . ."

"Um, well, that's not all," Prue said, looking guilty.

"Okay . . ." Piper said, dropping her briefcase again.

"Well, I'm going to have to hire eight models . . ."

"Actually, you don't!" Phoebe piped up, jumping out of her wicker chair.

"Excuse me?" Prue said, turning to eye her sister suspiciously.

"Nikos would be so perfect for this photo, trust me," Phoebe gushed. "And I'm sure he'd be willing to pose. I mean anything for the sake of art. *And*, I daresay, the sake of me."

"Whoa!" Piper said. "Things sure are swimming along quickly with you guys."

"I'm crazy about him!" Phoebe exclaimed, spinning around and flopping back into her chair. "But we haven't graduated past coffee dates. This is the perfect way to kick things up to the next level—a long photo shoot in my very own house. We could take breaks on the front porch . . . and maybe the couch . . ."

"Phoebe!" Prue and Piper burst out.

"Hey, a girl can daydream," Phoebe retorted. "So, what do you say, Prue? Let me ask Nikos to model for you, please, please, please!"

Prue sighed.

"Well, I was going to use professional models, but using Nikos *would* cut down on the cost . . ." Prue began. Then she glanced at Phoebe's mischievous, pleading face.

"Okay," she agreed. "Nikos it is. Now I only need to worry about seven models."

"Six!" Phoebe said, jumping back to her feet.

"Phoebe," Prue protested, "I think I can count, thank you."

"Why hire a model when you've got a perfectly willing sister?" Phoebe said, planting her fists on her slender hips. "Did I, or did I not, hear you tell me I was, quote, gorgeous, unquote just a few minutes ago."

"Man, did *I* miss a love fest," Piper quipped,

rolling her eyes and leaning against the living room doorjamb.

"Phoebe, I can't have you slobbering all over Nikos while I'm working," Prue said. "With that many models, the shoot's going to take all day as it is."

"Slobbering!" Phoebe said. "I so resent that. I can be as professional as the next supermodel, if not as skinny. I swear I'll be good. I can be Hera, and Nikos can be the other one, whatshisname."

"Zeus," Piper said dryly. "As in the king of the gods."

"Yeah, him," Phoebe said absently. "It'll be perfect."

"I don't know . . ." Prue said, biting her lip.

"How about this," Phoebe bargained. "I go to school on a college campus filled with beautiful young things. *I* can find you six other models to round out the shoot. Responsible babes only, I promise. Then you could *really* cut your costs. What better way to suck up to your editor?"

"In Phoebe's own warped way, she does have a point," Piper said, glancing at Prue.

Prue frowned and squinted at her youngest sister. Phoebe was famous in the Halliwell family for flaking out—always being late, always forgetting to gas up the car, always biting off more than she could chew. But ever since she'd moved back to the manor, she'd grown up. Prue really wanted to trust her. Finally, she nodded.

"Okay, okay," she said. "I know not to stand in your way when you want something, Phoebe. And it *would* help me make my deadline if you took care of hiring the models. But remember, I've got a lot riding on this. *Please* don't flake out on me!"

"I'm not even going to bother to take offense at that," Phoebe said, grinning excitedly. "If it'll get me closer to Nikos, I'll find the best darn hotties on campus. Your shoot is in the bag, Prue. Trust me." She flopped happily back into her wicker chair.

"Okay, well, you don't need *me*, then," Piper announced, scooping up her briefcase once more and heading for the front door. She was just reaching for the knob when Prue appeared in front of her. As in, appeared out of thin air. Then she stood at the door, her hands on her hips, blocking Piper's exit.

Piper rolled her eyes.

"Prue!" she called over her shoulder. "You know I hate it when you go astral in the house."

Prue shimmered into nothingness. Because, of course, that hadn't been Prue at all. It was merely her astral projection, a specter of herself that she could instantaneously shoot to other places. It was sort of like throwing your voice but with more oomph.

Prue stepped out of the living room and into the foyer, looking guilty.

"I couldn't let you leave," she said. "I have just one more little, tiny favor to ask of you."

"Uh-huh," Piper said, placing a hand on her hip.

"Well, Phoebe was right. As I said, this is going to be an all-day shoot, and well, I'll need to feed the models . . ."

"You want me to cook for you and eight models?" Piper asked.

"And I'll probably need a photographer's assistant, too," Prue said, scraping her toe on the parquet. "Please, Piper, it'll be fun! You told me you've been meaning to develop some new recipes for P3. Here's your chance. Besides, this is my big break. I need your support."

Piper bit her lip. Of course, she wanted to help Prue. But this just added to her feeling that her sisters were doing major things in their lives, while she was just on the sidelines . . . cooking dinner.

"Well, since I don't start work until the evening, I guess I can't say no," Piper said grudgingly.

"Thanks, sweetie," Prue said, giving Piper another hug. "What would I do without you?"

"I don't know, order pizza?" Piper said with a wink. Then she opened the stained-glass door and headed to work.

The next day the manor doorbell rang sharply at noon. Prue glanced in the foyer mirror as she hurried to answer it. She was glad she'd let Phoebe convince her to go with the hot-pink halter and turquoise satin capris. With her long black hair tied into a loose top-knot, she looked casual enough for lunch, but glam enough to let Mitchell know she was definitely interested.

When she opened the door, his face showed that he was clearly interested, too.

"Wow . . ." Mitchell breathed.

"Hi," Prue said, feeling herself blush again.

Mitchell stepped inside and said, "Prue, you look, amazing."

He gazed around the foyer at the antique grandfather clock and swooping walnut staircase, the overstuffed horsehair sofas, and the velvet chaise.

"And I've got to tell you, your house is almost as

breathtaking as you are," he said. "This is some place."

"It was my grandmother's house," Prue said, leaning against an ornately carved chair. "You could say she was *really* into antiques."

"Can I make a suggestion?" Mitchell said, strolling into the sunroom. "That Victorian architecture shoot you were talking about? You should do it right here. In this very room."

"I'm one step ahead of you," Prue said, following him. In the light of the sunroom, she could see the natural blond highlights in his hair. She also couldn't help but notice how nicely his gray shirt picked up the color in his eyes. "I've got a shoot scheduled here two days from now."

"You're kidding!" Mitchell said. "I should have known, Prue. You're so together. And you're clearly so talented."

Prue could feel warmth spread through her. Mitchell was incredible. With many guys, she'd write the compliment off as empty flattery. But Mitchell seemed so sincere. She couldn't wait to spend an entire lunch with him.

"So are you hungry?" Prue asked. "Lead the way to the restaurant."

In twenty minutes Prue and Mitchell were sitting at a very small table outside Bien Hoa, a tiny place in the Castro neighborhood. An elderly siver-haired woman walked across the deck to their table and served them glasses of sweet, milky iced tea.

"Your order?" she asked in a thick accent.

Mitchell began speaking to the woman in

Vietnamese. Prue's eyes widened. Apparently, Mitchell had done plenty of research before she'd met him in the library yesterday. She was impressed.

The elderly woman clearly felt the same way. When she heard Mitchell speak her native tongue, she responded with a huge smile and several minutes of excited chatter. Finally, she squeezed Mitchell's shoulder and hurried off.

"She's getting us the house specials," Mitchell said, turning to Prue with a smile. "She said to leave the ordering to her."

"Well, that's a good thing!" Prue laughed. "I wouldn't know what to order."

"You'll love the food. I promise," Mitchell said. "So, I want to hear more about your photography. How did you get started?"

Prue explained how she'd segued from the stuffy business of auctioning antiques to shooting for a hip, urban magazine.

"I guess I took quite a leap," she said with a shrug. "Sometimes I wonder how on earth I got here."

"I know the feeling," Mitchell said. "Let me tell you, when you travel as much as I do, sometimes you forget what city you've woken up in."

Prue laughed. "You know, we subscribe to *National Geographic*," she told Mitchell. "I flipped through some old issues and found the article you did about Prague's youth culture. It was so vivid, so fascinating. You're really good."

Mitchell looked into his tea glass. "Stop flattering me, Prue," he joked. "I'll get a swelled head."

But when he looked up at her, Prue could tell that he took enormous pride in his work. She felt so connected to Mitchell already. She'd finally met someone whose professional passion matched her own.

"Come on, tell me some tales from abroad," Prue urged him.

While Mitchell entertained her with vignettes about his travels, the silver-haired woman brought them two enormous bowls of steaming pho—a Vietnamese soup laden with fresh leafy vegetables and thinly sliced beef. Prue took a taste.

"Mmm!" she exclaimed. "It's delicious."

"Discovering cuisine like this is a nice perk of my job, isn't it?" Mitchell said.

"I'll say," Prue said, spooning up some more of her soup.

"Of course, there's nothing like capturing images on film, the way you do," Mitchell conceded. "A thousand words and all that . . . Hey! I just thought of something."

"Oh?"

"Have you hired an assistant for your photo shoot yet?" Mitchell asked.

Prue blinked.

"Actually no," she replied, taking a sip of the super-sweet tea. "In fact, I was planning on talking to my photo editor about that after lunch."

"Well, don't," Mitchell said. "I'll assist you. We'll call it our second date."

"You?" Prue said nervously. Oh no! she thought. How can I tactfully turn down Mitchell's offer?

After all, she was already using a bunch of amateur models. Having to correct Mitchell as he fumbled around her set was not going to make a great foundation for their relationship.

"Um, no offense, Mitchell, but you're a writer," she said carefully. "Do you know your way around a light meter?"

"I'm a *journalist*," Mitchell corrected her. "A product of Columbia Journalism School, in fact. And they're very old school there. Everybody learns photography and the basics of assisting shooters in the field."

Prue stared at Mitchell. Could this guy be any more perfect?

"You don't mind taking orders from your date?" she teased. "I run a pretty tight ship."

"Order away," Mitchell insisted. "I'd love to watch you work."

Prue pondered the idea for a moment as she ate some more pho.

"Okay," she agreed. "But you have to let 415 pay you. I insist."

"No way," Mitchell retorted. "I'm not in this for the money."

"Oh, really?" Prue said. "So what is it that's making you give up a day of your Vietnam research to hang around my house shooting pictures?"

"This . . ." Mitchell whispered. He leaned across their small table and planted a soft, warm kiss upon Prue's lips. Then he sat back in his chair, grinning adorably. Next thing Prue knew, *she* was leaning across the table and planting a smooch on *him*. His kiss was so warm, so intoxicating. It made her forget everything around them—the food, the sidewalk traffic near the restaurant—until the elderly woman bustled onto the deck with a plate of cold spring rolls.

As she walked up to their table, Prue and Mitchell sprang back into their seats. Both blushed slightly. But the woman just winked at Mitchell and pinched his cheek, saying something in Vietnamese.

When she left them alone, Prue felt herself still blushing.

"What did she say to you?" she gasped.

"She said, 'Don't mind the old lady. Kiss her some more!' " Mitchell told her.

"You're lying," Prue joked.

"No, I'm serious," Mitchell said, gazing into Prue's eyes. "And then she said, 'This fish, she's magic. Don't let her swim away!'"

Prue glanced quickly down at her soup bowl. Oh Mitchell, she thought wistfully, if you only knew.

CHAPTER
3

Phoebe! Aren't you up yet?"

Phoebe lifted her head from her pillow and squinted blearily at the door. Prue's indignant face was peeking through it.

"What time is it?" Phoebe croaked.

"Eight o'clock," Prue said, sounding exasperated. "The shoot's in two hours and there's so much to do."

"Uh . . . , there is?" Phoebe asked, hauling herself painfully to a sitting position and yawning widely. "Like beyond finding seven models, *which* I've done, and making sure everybody knows to be here at ten sharp, *which* I've also done. I think the only thing I haven't done for today's shoot is get enough beauty sleep, Prue."

Prue smiled ruefully and leaned against the door-jamb.

"I know. You totally came through for me,

Phoebs," she said. "I've been so busy getting costumes and putting the set together, I don't know
what I would have done if I'd had to take care of the
models, too."

"Gratitude accepted," Phoebe said, smiling sleep-
ily and flopping back onto her pillow.

"So, will Nikos be among these beautiful college
kids?" Prue asked.

"You know it," Phoebe said, propping her head on
her elbow and grinning at her sib. "He was way into
it when I asked him in class the other day. And get
this, he said, 'A Greek god? Me? You've got to be kidding!' Gorgeous, talented and modest, too. I *have* to
get this guy to be my boyfriend!"

"Well then, you *have* to get up, don't you?" Prue
said, wiggling her finger at the bed. Suddenly, the
fluffy duvet zipped off of Phoebe and landed in a
heap on the floor.

Phoebe stared at her bare toes. Then she glared
at her sister, who was grinning smugly from the
doorway.

"Telekinesis before breakfast, Prue?" Phoebe
growled, jumping out of bed. "You're *such* a witch."

"Tell me something I don't know." Prue giggled.
"Now, hurry up and shower. Then I need your help
with the costumes."

"Urgh, it's going to be a long day," Phoebe grumbled as she plodded to the bathroom. She glanced
into the mirror and gasped at the dark circles
beneath her eyes and her limp blond locks. Maybe
watching that two A.M. movie on TV hadn't been
such a good idea after all, especially since today was
her big chance with Nikos.

"You never know—this guy could be your future husband," she said to her reflection in the medicine cabinet mirror. "Don't blow it.

"Yeah, right," she said with a giggle. Then she hopped into the shower.

Downstairs, Prue rushed into the kitchen, carrying an armful of wispy dresses. Piper was just peeking into the oven, where three loaves of honey wheat bread were baking. Then she returned to the enormous pasta salad she was concocting.

"Piper, that smells fabulous," Prue said as she hung the gossamer robes over the kitchen chairs. "Now, I want to make sure I've got all our characters straight. So we'll have Zeus and Hera in the center, since they're the king and queen of the heavens, right?"

"Right," Piper said as she stirred some sun-dried tomatoes into her salad. "Zeus is lord of Mount Olympus. He's the big cheese. Then you've got Ares and Aphrodite, better known as Mars and Venus."

"You mean to tell me Mars and Venus actually had a love affair?" Prue said with a laugh.

"Oh, yeah," Piper said. "Aphrodite was actually married to Hephaestus, who was the only ugly god on Mount Olympus. So, she had an affair with Ares, the dashing god of war."

"Man, those gods and goddesses had their very own soap opera, didn't they?" Prue said, laying out some gold strappy sandals for the models.

"Don't even get me started," Piper said, rolling her eyes. "Okay, so then you'll have Artemis and

Apollo, who were twins. Artemis is the goddess of the hunt and Apollo is the god of music."

"So, he'll hold this lyre," Prue said, pulling a small, gold-painted harp out of a box of props she'd rented from a costume shop the day before.

"Perfect," Piper said. "And last but not least, you've got your edgy couple, Hades and Persephone."

"What's their story?" Prue asked.

Piper slipped on her oven mitts and began pulling her bread loaves out of the oven.

"Hades is the god of the underworld, but not by choice," she said over her shoulder. "He had two brothers—Zeus and Poseidon. When they came to power, they drew lots to see how to divide the world. Zeus won the draw and got the best position—king of the gods and ruler of the heavens. Next in line was Poseidon, who became lord of the sea. Last and least was Hades, who became king of the underworld, which also came to be called Hades. Eventually, he kidnapped a young goddess, Persephone, to be his wife. She would have been able to escape his clutches, but because she'd eaten one pomegranate seed while she was down under, she was doomed to spend half each year there. The rest of the time, she could come back to earth."

"Harsh," Prue said. "I love it for the photo though. I'll pick the darkest and most mysterious-looking guy in our group to play Hades. I can't wait to see what they all look like."

"Well, you won't have to wait too long," Piper said as the doorbell rang.

Prue glanced at her watch. "One of them is early!" she said incredulously. She dashed out of the kitchen.

"Ooh, I want to see the beautiful people!" Piper said, following Prue into the foyer—and forgetting to take off her oven mitts.

Prue threw the stained-glass door open and caught her breath. Standing before her was a tall, angular young man with a shock of glossy black curls and intense blue eyes. He wore distressed canvas carpenter pants and a tank top—an outfit that just screamed, "I'm an artist." He was also struggling with an enormous wooden box that stood on three rickety legs. A black velvet cloth hung off one end of the box.

"Whoa," Piper whispered as she peeked over Prue's shoulder. "Looks like we have our Hades. He's gorgeous!"

"Prue Halliwell?" the man said with a gleaming smile. "I'm Nikos. Phoebe's friend?"

"Come on in," Prue said, stepping back. She motioned at the brown box. "Is that what I think it is?"

Nikos placed his odd contraption in front of her.

"You got it—an old Brownie portrait box, circa 1904," he said. "My father—well, you could say he's a collector. He's got a lot of old stuff lurking around the basement. When I heard about your Victorian theme, I thought you might want to take a crack at this old camera."

"Would I!" Prue exclaimed. "This is perfect. Why didn't I think of it? A Victorian camera with glass plates instead of modern film. The photos shot with this camera will look like images from another age. This is just the thing I need to give me an edge over the competition. Nikos, how can I thank you?"

"Don't," the guy said with a grin. "Anything for a sister of Phoebe's."

"Well, how about a hello for Phoebe herself?" said a voice behind them. The trio spun around to behold the youngest Halliwell wearing a gossamer Greek gown and posing in the foyer doorway. The dress's high waist was tied with a crisscrossing of gold ribbons that matched the gold straps on her sandals. More gold ribbons were woven through Phoebe's hair, which was curled and piled upon the crown of her head. A serpent bangle around her biceps and a single pearl around her neck completed the look. Phoebe looked as though she'd stepped straight out of an ancient Greek frieze.

"Phoebe, you look awesome," Nikos said.

"You do!" Prue agreed. "Perfect for the photo."

"I found my costume in the kitchen and went ahead and changed," Phoebe explained as she brushed past Prue. Then she planted a kiss on Nikos's cheek.

"Hello, you Olympian god, you," she flirted.

"Oh, jeez," Piper muttered, rolling her eyes at Prue. "Let's go pick out an outfit for Hades, here."

Prue grabbed the camera, and she and Piper slipped out of the foyer, leaving Phoebe to make flirty eyes at her new sweetie.

"Well, this proves it," Nikos said to her. "You are beautiful in any time period—ancient Greek, Victorian, contemporary . . ."

"Aw, shucks," Phoebe said, batting her gold-dusted lashes. "Go on . . ."

"All right," Nikos said. "I will."

He leaned over.

He's going to kiss me, Phoebe thought, closing her eyes. My plan *so* worked . . .

Just then a chime sounded.

"Whoops," Nikos said, jerking backward. "Guess that's the doorbell."

"Guess so." Phoebe sighed. Irritated, she stalked to the door and threw it open. Standing on the porch was Chloe, a willowy blond girl with skin so pale, it was almost translucent. Her perfect, pouty lips were pursed into a self-important sneer. When Phoebe had seen this haughty babe on campus, she'd known she'd be perfect for Prue's photo. Of course, she *hadn't* known that Chloe would have a supermodel-size attitude. Phoebe sighed and rolled her eyes. What did I expect? she mused.

Next to Chloe was a very cute, muscular guy with spiky brown hair and a bulging bag of gear.

"Hi, I'm Mitchell," the man said, reaching out to shake Phoebe's hand. "I'll be Prue's assistant for the shoot."

Finally, Chloe deigned to speak, too.

"Hello, Phoebe," she drawled, stalking into the foyer. "I guess I'm in the right place. We *do* have hair and makeup, don't we?"

"Uh, that would be me," Phoebe said, motioning the girl into the kitchen. Then she glanced at Nikos and rolled her eyes. "Guess we have to get to work," she whispered to him.

"I'll remember where we left off," he whispered back. Then he winked.

O-*kay*, Phoebe thrilled inwardly. Back on plan.

An hour later four men and three women were lounging around the kitchen in gold-edged tunics, filmy dresses, and Grecian sandals. The kitchen table was littered with fake shields, lyres, and pan pipes. And the air was thick with the conversation of beautiful young things.

"So, I said to the prof, 'You can't give me an incomplete.' I mean, I had an *audition*," said Kurt, the buff blond playing Apollo.

"Mmmm, interesting," droned Madelaine, a stunning redhead in full Hera gear, who was munching one of Piper's canapés. "Do you think this hors d'oeuvre is fat-free?"

Phoebe, meanwhile, was hanging in the sunroom with Nikos and Mitchell. Mitchell was setting up light reflectors around the room. Nikos and Phoebe were simply flirting.

"I've got to say, Nikos, you've got lovely legs," Phoebe joked, eyeing her hottie's short tunic.

"I'll bet you say that to all the gods," he teased back.

Phoebe laughed. "Why, you're the only god I kno—"

"Phoebe!"

Phoebe jumped and turned around. Prue was standing next to the Victorian camera at the sunroom entrance. She was wearing baggy overalls and a dour expression.

"Prue!" Phoebe said with alarm.

"Prue . . ." Mitchell said with admiration.

"Hi, Mitchell," Prue said, trying to shoot a smile at her gorgeous "assistant" while she simultaneously glared at her sister.

"Um, is there a problem?" Phoebe asked, glancing through the living room to the model-filled kitchen. "The natives certainly look happy."

"Yes, well, did you notice that we're one native short?" Prue hissed. Inside she was seething. I knew

I shouldn't have trusted Phoebe, she thought. Of course, something was bound to go wrong.

"That can't be," Phoebe said weakly, lurching to her feet. "I confirmed with everyone."

"Well, one of the women didn't show," Prue said curtly. "And we're in big trouble."

Piper walked into the room holding a tray.

"Phoebe, you'll try my crab fritters, won't you?" she said, offering a savory-smelling appetizer. "None of the models will touch them. It's a deep-fried thing."

"Not now, Piper," Phoebe began. "We have a cri— Hey. . . . Piper." Phoebe suddenly smiled at her sister. Prue's eyes widened as she read Phoebe's mind. Then she turned and smiled her own sweet smile.

"Piper . . ." she began.

Piper's jaw dropped. Then she spun around and headed right back to the kitchen.

"Oh no," she called over her shoulder. "I recognize that tone of voice. You guys are going to ask me for another favor. And I can *tell* I'm not going to like it."

"But you'd look so pretty in this," Prue said, showing her the last costume—a low-cut, sheer sheath.

"And . . . you love Greek food!" Phoebe stammered.

"Desperate, Phoebs," Piper said, plopping her tray on the counter. "Really desperate."

"You're right," Prue cut in. "We are desperate. One of the models didn't show up, and if you won't fill in for her, my whole tableau will be ruined. And my one chance at the 415 cover? Dashed!"

"Okay, okay," Piper said. "I'll do it. Just please,

put me in the back of the crowd. This is sooo embarrassing."

In just a few minutes, the models were assembled on the antique furnishings in the sunroom. With Mitchell's help, Prue arranged them in classical poses. Joey, the guy playing Ares, held a spear aloft and looked fierce while Aphrodite—otherwise known as Piper—draped herself awkwardly over his shoulder. She yanked at the hem of her short tunic and hunched her shoulders.

To depict Persephone, the captive bride of Hades, Prue had Phoebe lay a hand across her forehead and turn her back to Nikos, playing the god of the underworld.

"Uh, Phoebe," Mitchell whispered to her, "are you sure you should be sitting so close to Hades? I mean, you're not supposed to really like him in this scenario."

"Shhh," Phoebe said, winking at Mitchell and sidling even closer to Nikos.

Mitchell winked back and held a light meter up to Phoebe's face.

"It's at seven point four, Prue," he announced.

"Great," Prue said, ducking under the velvet drape of the antique camera. "Okay, looking good. Everybody ready?"

"Actually, I am *very* uncomfortable," said Chloe, the petulant blond who was playing Artemis. She was aiming an arrow at the wall and giving the camera a sultry stare. "Those canapés were much too salty. I'm parched. May I have some spring water please? Make sure it's spring, *not* mineral."

Prue planted her fists on her hips. She was about to tell the prima donna just what she could do with her spring, not mineral, water, when Mitchell placed a calming hand on her shoulder.

"Of course, I'll get you some water," he told Chloe. "Evian or Pellegrino?"

"Evian," Chloe ordered.

"You're a saint," Prue whispered to Mitchell with a grin.

"What are assistants for?" he whispered back. Then he headed into the kitchen to get the water.

Prue ducked back under her velvet drape. She thrilled inside. This was going to be a gorgeous shot. She could already envision it on *415*'s cover.

"Looks almost perfect," she called from beneath the drape. "Now, Phoebe, if you'll just unpeel yourself from Nikos, and Piper, if you could try to look a little less stricken, I'll take our first shot."

"Who died and made her Annie Leibovitz?" Piper muttered through gritted teeth while Phoebe stifled a snort of laughter.

"Okay!" Prue announced, holding her antique flashbulb aloft. "Here we go. One . . . two . . . three!"

Psffftttt!

Piper saw the flash go off and then, for a moment, she was utterly blinded. When the bright light subsided, she squinted painfully. Then she looked down and gasped. "Ares" had slithered out of her embrace and collapsed onto the floor at her feet.

"Prue. . . ." Piper started to say. She looked around her. Nikos, Chloe . . . all the pretty young things had slumped over in heaps. Only Phoebe sat upright, blinking in confusion.

Prue emerged from the drape looking panicked.

"What happened?" she gasped, rushing forward and kneeling over Kurt/Apollo. She jostled him lightly and put her face close to his.

"He's breathing," Prue said.

"So is Hera over here," Piper said, lifting Madelaine's limp hand and dropping it into her lap. "In fact, she's snoring!"

Phoebe peered at Nikos. "He looks so peaceful," she said. "They've all just fallen asleep."

"Yeah," Prue said, nudging Kurt again. He kept on snoozing away. "They've fallen and they can't get up."

"One Evian, *with* a straw, coming up," called a voice from the kitchen.

"Mitchell!" Phoebe gasped.

Piper could see Mitchell's boot toe stepping into the living room. Before she could think twice, she waved her hands in front of her. The boot toe, and the rest of Mitchell, froze in place. The sound of Hera's snoring, along with the ticking of their grandfather clock halted, too. Time was stopped, for the moment anyway.

"Good call, Piper," Phoebe said, lurching to her feet. "I don't know what this is, but it's definitely something supernatural."

"Which means Mitchell had better not find out about it," Prue finished for her. She rushed to the wooden archway that separated the sunroom from the living room and unhooked the pale green curtain from its usual spot, tucked against the door frame. Then she zipped the curtain across the brass rod, hiding the heap of sleeping models, as well as Phoebe and Piper, from Mitchell's view.

Just in time, too. The minute Prue shimmied the curtain into place, Mitchell unfroze. He stepped into the living room, holding the bottle of water.

He looked from the curtain to Prue and back to the curtain.

"Ten-minute break already?" he said. "I thought you said you ran a tight ship."

"Uhhhh," Prue stalled.

"Broken spaghetti strap," Phoebe shrieked from behind the curtain. "We've got a costume crisis here. We're not decent. So don't peek!"

"Exactly!" Prue blurted. Inwardly, she groaned. Leave it to Phoebe to come up with the most lurid lie imaginable. But she couldn't back out of it now.

"I can't believe how flimsy those costumes are," Prue complained, shoving Mitchell into the foyer. "In fact, I'm going to take them back to the costume shop right now and demand some new ones."

"Let me do that for you," Mitchell protested. "I'm the assistant after all."

"No!" shouted Piper and Phoebe from the sunroom.

"Uh . . . they're right," Prue stammered. "My name is on the order. I'll just have to do it myself, and we'll have to resume the shoot this afternoon."

She opened the front door.

"So, I really can't make you wait around here," she said, nudging Mitchell onto the front porch. "But you were so great this morning. Thanks for your help. Couldn't have done it without you. Good-bye!"

"Wait," Mitchell cried, blocking the door as Prue tried to slam it shut. "What about the rest of the shoot this afternoon? Won't you need an assistant?"

"You know what?" Prue said, feeling regret as

she gave Mitchell this necessary brush-off. "You're a fabulous assistant, but I think I just work better solo."

"Well . . ." Mitchell sputtered, "that's understandable, I guess."

"Great!" Prue said. Then she tried to slam the door again.

"Prue!" Mitchell blurted, stopping her once more. "If you don't want me to be your assistant, at least let me take you to dinner tomorrow. I really want to see you again."

"Fine!" Prue blurted, feeling panic and elation at the same time. Maybe she could get through this whole snafu without blowing it with Mitchell. "Why don't you come by at eight. See you then!"

With that, Prue succeeded in slamming the door. She spun around and leaned back against it, breathing hard. She *hated* these awkward witch-mortal moments!

Sighing, Prue stalked back into the living room and yanked open the curtain. Piper and Phoebe were sitting on the floor, staring at the pile of slumbering babes.

"We've checked on them all," Piper said. "They seem fine. They're just in a deep, deep sleep."

"So much for my big after-the-shoot plans with Nikos," Phoebe said morosely, poking at her honey's babealicious but inert body.

"And so much for my 415 cover, thanks to your boyfriend, here!" Prue said angrily. She glared at Phoebe. "What do you think he is? Demon or warlock? It's so hard to tell with that buff disguise."

"How do you know it was Nikos's fault?" Phoebe

protested, leaping to her sandaled feet. "The camera wasn't even his. He said he found it in his father's basement. It could have come from anywhere."

"Right, Phoebe," Prue said, fuming as she briskly yanked the negative plate out of the camera and put it into a protective metal box. "Right now I don't care what he is. All I know is, *you* brought him here and *he* brought a cursed camera with him. And now we've got six people under some sort of spell *in our living room!* My ruined photo shoot is nothing compared to the trouble we're in if we can't revive these models."

"She's right," Piper said, tugging at her too-short tunic and biting her lip.

"I just don't get it," Phoebe said, walking up to the camera. "It looks like an ordinary old musty antique to me."

She peered at the camera and laid her hand on top of it. Instantly, a shock passed through her body. She gasped and squeezed her eyes shut. It was one of her premonitions—she could feel it coming on.

She was walking through a dark, swampy forest. She looked down and saw her gold-sandaled feet squishing along a muddy, moist trail. The trees loomed around her like sinister skeletons, and in the distance she could hear anguished ghostly cries.

She gazed around but saw nothing but mist. And wait—there were also a few ghostly wisps, darting behind the trees. She was terrified, but also felt as though this place were somehow . . . familiar.

At that moment Phoebe felt her mind whoosh away from the scene. She blinked to see her sisters hovering over her, looking worried. She'd slumped to the floor near the camera.

"A premonition?" Piper asked.

"Uh-huh," Phoebe said breathlessly. "I was in a swamp—I have no idea where. But something makes me think our models have been taken there."

Prue and Piper glanced at each other.

"*Book of Shadows?*" Prue prompted.

"You took the words right out of my mouth," Piper answered.

With that, the three sisters rushed up the stairs to the attic.

The attic was filled with old horsehair sofas and cane chairs, yellowed dress forms, and rusty birdcages. But the center of the room had been cleared of clutter. This was where an old wood bookstand stood, holding the enormous leather-bound *Book of Shadows.*

The sisters leaped upon the tome. Phoebe began flipping through its weathered vellum pages.

"Let's see . . ." she muttered. "Pictures, sleep spells, camera . . . Ah! Cameras."

Piper and Prue leaned over Phoebe's shoulders as she read out loud.

" 'Primitive cultures have long been mocked for their belief that a camera will steal one's soul,' " she said. " 'Little do most mortals know that cameras are classic portals to points beyond.' "

"Points beyond?" Piper said. "And that would be where exactly?"

"You know the *BOS*," Prue said, sighing. "Always cryptic."

" 'The soul is captured by an energy vortex in a

spellbound camera,' " Phoebe continued. " 'It must be retrieved through the same portal.' "

"It sounds like we can travel through the camera to retrieve the souls of our models," Prue said.

"But we weren't zapped the first time the shutter closed," Piper pointed out. "It must have been our powers that protected us. So how are we going to make it work this time?"

The sisters eyed one another. Then all three blurted, "Spell."

"Yup, let's see what we can whip up," Phoebe said, flipping through the book again. "Okay, how about this one?"

" 'For an instant may we be ordinary mortals three,' " Piper read.

" 'Take us where we want to go, then back to our powers let us go,' " Prue finished. Piper quickly scribbled the lines on a scrap of paper.

"I think that'll do it," Phoebe said, slamming *The Book of Shadows* shut. "Let's go downstairs and kick it into gear."

"*Grrrrrrrrr.*"

"Wait a minute," Piper said, glancing over her shoulder into the shadowy recesses of the attic. "Did you hear that?"

"What?" Prue asked, heading for the stairs.

"*GRRRRRRRRRRR!*"

"Okay, wait a minute," Phoebe said, her voice shaking. She grabbed Piper's arm. "I definitely heard that."

"*Grrrrr-OWR!*"

With another horrible growl, something leaped out of the farthest corner of the attic. In the dark gloom, Phoebe struggled to see the intruder. It was some kind of beast. It lunged closer. That's when Phoebe let out a bloodcurdling scream.

The beast was a ferocious, menacing dog. Its muscles rippled beneath a shiny black coat. Its razorlike claws dug into the attic's floorboards. And it snarled at the sisters with not one, not two, but three furious heads!

CHAPTER
4

Whoa!" Piper screamed, waving her hands before her in panic. The three-headed beast froze in midleap, just as one of its gaping sets of jaws was about to snap closed on her throat.

"Ooo-kay," Phoebe said, her voice trembling. "This is new."

Prue ran back up the stairs to join her sisters. She gasped at the three sets of vicious teeth, the six bloodshot yellow eyes, and the bear-size muscular body.

"Suggestions?" she asked, staring at the other-worldly beast.

"Vanquish his butt!" Phoebe cried.

"But how?" Piper said, just as time unfroze and the dog landed before them, growling fiercely.

Prue waved her arm and caught the dog with an invisible fist, sending it flying across the attic. It crashed into a mirror, smashing the thing to smithereens. But the dog barely seemed injured. It shook its three heads and began running back to the witches.

"Grrr-ROWR!"

It pounced at Prue. She caught one of its throats with a roundhouse kick, knocking the dog away. Then she swung her arm and sent the creature crashing down the stairs. It hit the bottom of the stairwell with a thud.

"AAAAARRRP!" the dog yelped.

"Finally, an injury," Phoebe breathed. She quickly looked around for a refuge. Suddenly, she spied an old lamp. She'd brought it up to the attic a few weeks earlier because the electrical cord had frayed. It was a total fire hazard. She'd stashed it here, intending to get it fixed when she had more time.

"I'm not a physics major, but I have an idea," she said. Then she turned to Piper.

"You be the bait," she ordered, grabbing her sister and planting her in front of the stairwell.

"Hello?" Piper squeaked. "Did you just say bait?"

"Prue," Phoebe said, tossing her sib the end of the lamp's electrical cord. "Plug this in."

Prue followed Phoebe's orders. Phoebe grabbed at the rubber around the cord and ripped at it, exposing a length of naked wire. Then she gripped the lamp with all her strength and stretched the cord across the top of the stairwell.

"Grrrrrrrr."

The menacing sound was coming from the bottom step of the attic stairs.

"Phoebs," Piper said shakily, "I don't like the sound of that."

"Don't move," Phoebe ordered. "But be ready to go into freeze mode if you have to."

"GRRRRRRRRR!"

"Here he comes," Piper yelled.

Phoebe could hear the giant dog lumbering up the attic stairs—snarling and huffing and lunging at her sister.

"Phoebe!" Piper screamed.

"Now!" Phoebe yelled. She pulled the lamp up just as the beast leaped out of the stairwell. The exposed wire caught it across the chest and burst into flames.

The dog's three heads rolled in agony, and it howled with pain as the wire seared its flesh. As sparks flew off its body, the sisters scrambled out of the way.

With a few more horrible howls, the dog suddenly exploded in a fiery blast. Phoebe threw herself to the floor. When she finally looked up, the creature was gone. All she could see was a poof of acrid black smoke. Beyond it, her sisters were cowering in the corner. They stood up shakily and ran to Phoebe's side.

"You okay?" Prue asked.

Phoebe nodded breathlessly.

"Let's get to that camera," Piper declared, leading the way down the attic stairs.

As they rushed through the upstairs hallway and clattered down the main staircase, Prue said, "I'm going to have to rig up a shutter release cord so we can all be in front of the lens when I take the picture. That way we'll all be zapped at the same time."

"You do that while I check on the sleeping beauties," Phoebe said. She ran into the sunroom and began examining the pile of unconscious models.

"And I've got the spell," Piper said, waving the piece of paper where she'd written it down.

Prue had just located the long shutter release cord in her camera bag when she heard a sound. A horrible sound.

"Ca-caw, ca-CAW!"

A chill skittered down her spine. And then she looked up.

"Piper, Phoebe!" she screamed, leaping to her feet.

Perched on top of the camera was a creature even more grotesque, if possible, than the three-headed dog. It had a woman's head—beak-nosed, lipless, and chalky white. It had a scaly human torso, as well. But where there should have been arms were flapping wings. Instead of legs, the animal had a hawk's talons and a long feathery tail.

"What the—" Piper blurted.

Prue didn't stop to wonder what this creature was. Instead, she just flung her arm out, zinging it off the camera. The beast emitted a dreadful screech. But before it could crash into the wall, it began flapping its wings. And then it flew right out of Prue's telekinetic strike! It swooped around the ceiling, screeching down at the sisters.

"Watch the models," Prue shrieked as the creature swooped down near the sleeping forms in the sunroom. Piper rushed to protect the models, but the creature passed over them, ignoring them completely. Instead, it hissed at Piper and clawed at her, missing her eyes by an inch.

"I don't think it's interested in them," Piper screamed.

"No," Prue agreed, ducking to miss a swipe of the

creature's talons. "I think it's safe to say this thing's here for us."

"I think this is a job for super-Phoebe," Phoebe piped up from the other side of the room. Piper and Prue spun around to see their sister hovering in the air across the room from the bird-woman.

The creature let out a terrifying screech and shot through the air toward the youngest witch. Phoebe was ready with a dizzying series of airborne karate chops. The creature slapped at her with its wings, but Phoebe spun in the air, kicking them away with powerful thrusts of her feet. She swooped to avoid the creature's flying talons and spun to duck its powerful tail.

"She's really getting the hang of that flying thing," Piper said to Prue.

"You know it!" Prue replied. Then she yelled to Phoebe, "Ready for me to take over?"

"On the count of three," Phoebe yelled, swiping at the creature for all she was worth. "One . . . two . . ."

She spun around twice and punched the creature in the face as she screamed, "Three!"

The bird-woman careened into the foyer where Prue was waiting. She waved her arms at the creature, pummeling it with a powerful telekinetic thrust. Weakened and screeching, the horrible beast slammed into the wall. The blow was enough to make it explode into a cloud of feathers and ash.

Phoebe plummeted to the floor with a thud.

"Ooooh," she groaned. "Flying's getting easier, but landing is still tricky."

"Let's get to the camera before anything else pops up," Piper said. "Phoebs, come with me over here."

Piper and Phoebe positioned themselves in front of the camera lens while Prue rushed to attach the shutter release cord to the camera.

"This thing is so old, I hope I can get it attached," she muttered, struggling with the camera.

"Pruuuue," Phoebe said, eyeing the living room corner, where the air was beginning to waver and shimmer. "I think we've got a new visitor dropping in on us!"

"Almost there," Prue grunted, screwing the cable onto a tiny appendage on the camera.

"Hurry," Piper shrieked.

"Got it," Prue announced, just as a nine-headed serpent appeared in the corner, hissing wildly.

"Say the spell," Prue yelled as she leaped to join her sisters in front of the camera. They grabbed one another's hands.

"For an instant may we be," the sisters chanted, "ordinary mortals three. . . ."

"Hisssssssss."

"Take us where we want to go . . ."

The serpent began to slither across the room.

"Then back to our powers let us go!"

Uttering the last word of the spell left them, for an instant, without their magic powers—just when a lethal snake was lunging at them.

"Now!" Phoebe and Piper screamed.

Prue hit the shutter button and cringed as the flashbulb exploded. Then she felt her body crumpling to the ground as her mind was pulled down a dark, swirling, roaring tunnel. She could feel her sisters' hands in hers, which lessened her fear for an instant.

Then everything went black.

*   *   *

Phoebe blinked and shook her head. She was on her hands and knees, and she was sure she'd lost consciousness for a second. Glancing up quickly, she saw Prue and Piper nearby, looking as bleary as she felt.

Phoebe lurched to her feet and shivered. She was standing in a patch of oozing mud, and her filmy Grecian dress was smeared with damp sludge. Her feet sank into the ground with a sickening squelch.

"Uch," Piper said, lifting her own dripping foot out of the muck. "Where are we?"

"I don't know," Phoebe said, looking around. They were surrounded by gray, leafless, looming trees. Through the misty gloom, Phoebe thought she could see some wispy white bodies flitting in and out of the tree branches. Were they ghosts?

And in the distance, she could just make out a desiccated mansion, crumbling and overrun by vines.

"Wait a minute!" she exclaimed. "I *do* know where we are. Well, sort of. This is the scene from my premonition."

With a gasp, Phoebe realized something else. She'd just realized why her premonition had felt so familiar: She was standing inside Nikos's painting! Everything was here—the ghostly figures, the crumbling manse, the gnarled trees.

She started to tell her sisters about the painting, but something made her swallow the words back. She had no idea what all this meant, but she *did* know that Prue was majorly suspicious of Nikos.

Knowing about his painting would only feed that suspicion.

But Phoebe felt sure that Nikos wasn't responsible for this fix. He couldn't be. He was so great! And sweet! And cute!

This all has to be some sort of fluke, she thought stubbornly. Maybe his painting was a trigger . . . or something. Anyway, if we don't get out of this muck and find some clues, we'll never know either way.

She squinted into the woods and scanned the landscape for something, anything that would point her in the right direction. Piper sloshed up next to her.

"Where on earth, or well, wherever we are, do you think we should go?" she asked.

Phoebe shrugged, already feeling guilty for not clueing her sibs into her extra information.

"Hey," Prue called from a few yards away. She was squinting through a thicket. "Did you see that?"

Piper and Phoebe squished over to her.

"See what?" Piper asked, following Prue's gaze.

"I saw a flash of light," Prue said excitedly. "Just a glimmer. Then it faded out, almost like a firefly."

Phoebe peered through the gloom.

"Are you sure that wasn't wishful thinking, Prue?" she said, rubbing her hands over the goose bumps on her arms. "After all, this isn't exactly hot summer firefly weather."

Suddenly, she saw a faint light wink through the trees.

"There it is!" she cried. "Is that the light you saw, Prue?"

"Yup," Prue said.

"I saw it, too," Piper said.

"Well, looks like we've got something to go on," Phoebe said, plunging forward. "Let's move!"

The sisters spent about an hour slogging through the swampy wood. Owls and bats swooped down around them, making them cringe and squeal. Their hair kept getting caught in thorny shrubs. Foul-smelling, cold muck—sap or slime or who knew what—dripped off tree branches, landing creepily on their heads and bare shoulders.

"This is the nastiest experience I've had since I took the P3 staff on one of those wilderness retreats," Piper complained, feeling her tunic catch—and tear—on a prickle bush.

"Don't forget about the time you lost your retainer in the Dumpster," Phoebe grunted as she tiptoed through a bubbling brown stream. "That might have been a *smidge* nastier."

"Come on, you guys," Prue said, climbing over a craggy boulder. "We're almost there. I just saw the light flash again, and it was much closer."

After another half mile or so of their painful hike, the sisters emerged onto a sandy beach.

"Is that a lake?" Phoebe asked, squinting at a large body of water in front of them. It was enshrouded in a smelly, soupy fog.

"It's a river," Piper said, pointing at the sluggish current. Brackish yellow waves bubbled onto the sand, lapping their toes.

"Yuck!" Prue exclaimed, jumping backward.

"Now the big question is, where's our firefly friend?" Piper said, shivering and gazing into the haze.

"And an even bigger question," Prue said, "is how do we get across this river? I don't see a bridge anywhere."

Suddenly, a long, narrow boat drifted lazily out of the fog. From a stake in the boat's stern hung a glass lamp with a flickering flame inside. Standing next to it, a hooded figure in a long black robe was poling the boat toward them.

"Speak of the devil," Phoebe said, nervously. "Or . . . whomever."

The sisters stared as the small boat floated creepily toward them. Finally, it hit the beach with a gentle thud. The hooded figure stood silently.

"You think he's gonna say anything?" Phoebe whispered.

"Maybe he's waiting for us to make the first move," Prue whispered back. "Piper, get ready to freeze him if he does anything fishy."

"Right," Piper quavered.

Then Prue stepped forward, positioning herself at the end of the boat. She tried to peer at the figure's face, but his long black hood kept it in shadows.

"Can you tell us what's on the other side of this river?" Prue asked.

The figure shook his head back and forth.

Prue cast a nervous glance back at her sisters. Then she turned back to the boatman.

"Well . . . can you point us to a bridge?"

Again, the man shook his head.

"Okay," Phoebe cut in. "How about taking us across the river yourself?"

Finally, the robed man nodded.

"Phoebe," Piper whispered "are you sure that's a

good idea. Remember what our mother always told us—never accept rides from strangers?"

"What choice do we have?" Phoebe whispered back. She started to climb into the boat. But the ferryman stopped her, holding out his hand.

Phoebe looked at it and recoiled with a gasp.

The hand was . . . rotting! The flesh was dirty, moldering, and oozing with sores. The nails were cracked and bloody. And Phoebe could detect a musty, disgusting odor wafting from the man's body. It was the smell of death. The ferryman seemed to be walking a fine line between life and the grave. She gagged.

The man's hand opened, as though he was waiting for Phoebe to hand him something.

"Uch!" she gasped, grabbing onto her sisters. She stared as the ferryman reached up and pulled back his hood. Beneath it was a gruesome face. The man's nose was half eaten away. Through his dirty, matted beard, Phoebe could see jagged brown teeth. His eyes were blank and blackened. Fleas and lice were visibly squirming in his long mane of hair.

Piper screamed. Then she felt herself go dizzy. Suddenly, all the pieces of this horrible day were falling into place. She clutched at her sisters and exclaimed, "I . . . I know who he is. That's Charon!"

"Charon," Prue breathed, staring at the living skeleton. "Okay, and he would be who?"

"This all makes sense now," Piper said. "The three-headed dog in the attic? That was Cerberus, a vicious guard dog from the Hercules legend. And the bird-woman was a Harpy—another creature from Greek mythology."

"And that snake thing with the zillion heads that was materializing in the living room when we left?" Phoebe asked.

"The Hydra," Piper said. "Definitely the Hydra."

"This still doesn't explain who Charon is," Prue whispered urgently.

"Charon is the ferryman who takes people across the River Acheron," Piper said in a trembling voice. "Dead people, that is."

"Dead people?" Prue whispered. "What is this River Acheron anyway?"

"It's the river of souls," Piper whispered, going white and clutching her sisters harder. "It's the entrance to the underworld. We're . . . we're in Hades!"

CHAPTER 5

As Piper uttered the horrible truth—that the sisters had been zapped to the underworld called Hades—Phoebe felt a chill course through her body. She lifted a trembling finger to the side of her throat. When she felt her pulse pounding away, she sighed with relief.

"Just checking," she whispered to her sisters. "Still alive."

"Uh, Piper . . ." Prue said, pointing at Charon. "What's he doing?"

The grisly figure was thrusting his oozing, open hand toward Prue.

"Oh, I know this," Piper said, putting a finger to her temple. "He wants us to pay the fare. Charon won't take anybody across the River Acheron without the proper fare. In ancient Greece, people were buried with coins to pay him."

"Charming history lesson," Phoebe muttered, patting her thin and pocketless Grecian robe. "But I seem to have left my wallet in the real world."

Prue searched the pockets of her overalls.

"I don't have so much as a quarter," she whispered desperately.

"That wouldn't be any good anyway," Piper whispered. "If I remember my classics class, the fare was one obol."

"Okay," Prue said dryly. "I don't know what an obol even is, but I know we don't have one. So what are we going to do?"

With a gruesome moist sound, Charon lifted his arm. He pointed a dirt-smeared finger at Phoebe's neck.

"What's he want?" Phoebe asked, trembling.

Piper followed Charon's gaze. At Phoebe's throat hung a single pearl on a delicate gold chain.

"I think he's saying he'll accept your necklace as the fare," Piper said with a gulp.

"But I love this necklace!" Phoebe complained, clapping her hand over it. She plucked the fake gold laurel wreath out of Piper's hair and offered it to the ferry driver instead. He shook his long, shaggy mane and pointed again at Phoebe's beautiful necklace.

"I guess you can't con Charon," she said ruefully. "Oh, all right."

Phoebe unclasped her necklace and deposited it into Charon's decaying palm. Then she climbed into the boat and reached to help Prue and Piper in. Charon used his long pole to turn the boat around. And then the Halliwell sisters plunged into the mist of the River Acheron.

In only a few minutes, they felt the boat scrape onto the opposite shore. Piper looked up at Charon. The skeleton was pointing to their left.

"I guess he would know where to go," Phoebe said. "He's obviously been here a while."

The sisters set off down a swampy road along the river, gazing around curiously. But all they saw were more dreary, looming trees.

"Forest to the right of us and fog river to the left of us," Prue muttered. "I wonder where we could be heading. It feels like the middle of nowhere."

Suddenly, the tepid wind changed and a burst of musty-smelling fog rolled off the River Acheron, drowning the girls in mist.

"Make that fog all around us," Piper said, waving her hands in front of her face. "Smelly fog, too!"

The sisters fanned irritably at the moist air and pressed on.

Eventually, the fog cleared and the sisters looked around again. They were still in the withered, awful forest. As they walked, the trees occasionally thinned out to reveal wizened fields, black streams that smelled of curdled milk, and every once in a while, an abandoned, dreary shack—small and dilapidated. There was no greenery, no sign of life. In every house they passed, the windows were eerily darkened. A chilly breeze whistled through their ears.

"Have you noticed how everything here is so dark and gray," Phoebe said. "Those shacks are the color of driftwood . . ."

"Just like the soil," Prue said, kicking at the road.

"Just like the trees," Piper said, glancing around and shivering. Her steps were getting sluggish.

"Oh, the monotony," Phoebe complained, trudging along.

"Stop complaining, you guy-guy-aaaaaaahs," Prue said, losing her words in a wide yawn.

"I'm not complaining," Piper mumbled. "I'm . . . just . . . tired."

Phoebe slumped to a stump at the side of the road and sat down.

"Just . . . a minute's rest. . . ." She yawned. "That's all I need."

Piper collapsed against Phoebe, leaning her head on her knee.

"Good idea," she murmured, closing her eyes. In an instant, they were both asleep.

Prue stood in the road, staring at her snoozing sisters, blinking hard and trying not to succumb to slumber herself. This . . . isn't . . . right, she thought slowly to herself. Why so . . . sleepy? I feel like . . . I've . . . been drugged.

Prue's blue eyes widened slightly. Drugged. That must be it. She took a stumbling step toward Piper and Phoebe.

"Wake . . . up," she whispered weakly. "Drugged . . . we've been drugged . . . a trick . . . I think maybe . . . that fog . . . off the river . . ."

But Prue could barely hold her eyes open. She slumped to her knees at Phoebe's feet. She was just about to give in to her weariness when she heard a sound in the distance.

"Ah-ha-ha-ha-ha!"

"Wha . . . ?" Prue whispered.

"AH-ha-ha-ha-ha!"

Her eyes flew open. She'd definitely heard that. A distant, menacing cackle.

"Piper," she rasped. "Phoebe, wake up!"

She shook her sisters' shoulders.

"What!" Piper said with a scowl, her brown eyes popping open.

"Sleepin'," Phoebe murmured, batting Prue's hand away. "Mmmmfffff."

"AH-HA-HA-HA-HAAAAAAA!"

"Prue," Piper said, fully awake now. "What was that?"

"I don't know, and I don't want to know," Prue said, lurching herself to her feet. She felt her head spin. "We've got to get out of here."

Piper hauled herself up, too.

"Ugh," she groaned. "I feel like my brain's been replaced with cotton."

"Me, too," Prue said. "But we've got to move. Get Phoebe up!"

Piper was just reaching for the snoozing Phoebe when they heard a clatter of hooves in a new thicket of trees up ahead. The sinister cackle rang through the air again—it was much closer now.

"Okay," Prue demanded, "what kind of horse laughs like that?"

"That kind!" Piper screamed, pointing at a bank of trees. An animal—or was it a man?—had just burst through a line of shrubs, spraying twigs and thorns everywhere.

"Oh no," Piper said, "it's a centaur. Half man, half horse. They're like the worst rabble-rousers in all of Greek mythology."

Prue stared at the creature. It looked like an ordinary brown horse from the waist down. Four hoofed legs, muscular flanks, and a brushy tail. But where a horse's head and waist should have been, she instead saw a man's bare torso. He was swarthy and hairy, with a shock of black curls and bushy, glowering eyebrows. The centaur galloped around them, stomping up swirls of dust and throwing back his head to laugh at them mockingly, flashing sharp brown little teeth.

"Yich!" Prue exclaimed. "How many of these messed-up creatures *are* there in these Greek myths anyway?" Prue demanded with a scowl.

"Too many!" Piper yelled, leaping at Phoebe. "Phoebs, wake up. Wake *up!*"

"What is it?" Phoebe said woozily, lifting her heavy head. She felt like she was emerging from a dark, dark cave. Her eyelids fluttered, struggling to open. Can't do it . . . she thought dully. Can't . . . wake . . . up.

Suddenly, something gripped her around the waist and swooped her into the air.

"Ooof!" she grunted.

Okay, *that* did the trick. Phoebe's eyes flew open. Then she shrieked in terror. She was slung across the back of a horse, pressed facedown into the animal's spine by a powerful human hand. And the horse was galloping away at full speed.

She swung her head around to peer up at her abductor.

"Aaaaaah!" she screamed. "You're no horse." She was appalled to be gazing at the hairy back of a man. Somehow, he was sprouting out of the front of this horse's body. The beast, who was reaching back to hold Phoebe captive, looked over his shoulder and grinned down at her.

"*Ah-ha-ha-ha-ha!*" he cackled, revealing a mouth full of rotten brown teeth. Then he took off into the gloom.

"Prue!" Phoebe screamed. "Piper! Save me!"

Prue and Piper gazed after their sister as she was carried off by the centaur. Piper waved her arms in the air, but the beast was too far away. She couldn't freeze him. She looked at Prue with panic in her eyes.

"There's nothing to do but chase him down!" she yelled. The sisters took off at a sprint.

"Pruuuuuue!" they heard Phoebe wail in the distance.

"*Ah-ha-ha-ha-ha!*" the centaur cackled.

"We're coming," Piper gasped.

But after about two minutes of hard sprinting, Prue and Piper began to tire.

"Can't . . . run . . . anymore," Prue gasped. "Of all the times . . . for me . . . to slack . . . off at aerobics."

"Come on!" Piper screeched, stumbling through the trees.

"No," Prue said, stumbling to a halt. "I have a better idea."

With that, her head drooped and her body slumped. Piper stared at her sister and bit her lip. She could tell Prue was in astral projection mode. She just hoped she could throw herself to wherever the centaur had disappeared with Phoebe.

Phoebe thought she was going to throw up. The horse-man was bouncing her so hard, she could barely see straight. That's why she was sure she was hallucinating when she saw her sister step out from behind a tree—and right into the galloping beast's path.

"Prue, watch out," she screamed.

"Aaaaack!" the creature bellowed, wheeling out of Prue's path just before he crashed into her. He began galloping in the opposite direction.

Somehow, Prue appeared again, standing directly in front of the beast's clattering hooves. She had her hands planted on her hips, and she was glaring at the creature.

That's when Phoebe realized that Prue had projected her image into the woods to save her.

The centaur was freaking. Every time he wheeled around, there was Prue, planted in his path with a glare on. When she'd disappeared and reappeared four times, the horse-man finally reared up on his hind legs, bellowing in fear.

"Whoooooa!" Phoebe screamed as she was thrown from his back. She landed with a thud in a pile of mulch.

The centaur cried out again and galloped off into the woods. In a moment, his hoofbeats died away. He was gone. Phoebe stumbled to her feet, rubbing her backside. She looked down at herself—her dress was in tatters, but all her bones seemed to be intact.

"Thanks, sis!" she said to Prue. But Prue just looked at her blankly and then, with a shimmer of light, disappeared.

"Oh, right. I almost forgot that was astral Prue," Phoebe said. Then she cupped her hands around her mouth and yelled. "Hellĺooooo!"

"Phoebe?" It was Piper, yelling in the distance.

"Over here!" Phoebe called into the gloom. She kept yelling until her sisters crashed through the brush and found her.

"My hero!" Phoebe cried, rushing over to give Prue a hug. "What was that horrible thing?"

"A centaur," Piper explained. "Half man, half horse. They have a nasty reputation. My guess is he was doing somebody else's bidding."

"But who?" Phoebe wondered.

"Let's keep moving," Prue said, shaking the last of the fog out of her head. "Hopefully we'll find out soon."

"Okay, we've totally lost that road," Piper said, frowning and looking around. All they could see was more murky darkness and more trees in every direction. "Which way?"

"How about we take the *opposite* direction from the centaur," Phoebe suggested.

"Good a plan as any," Prue said, nodding grimly.

The sisters forged ahead through the brush. They plodded silently, until they emerged into a glade, a circular clearing bisected by a stream.

"Let's follow the water," Piper said. "That's got to lead to something."

Prue and Phoebe shrugged and followed her lead. The stream curved and twisted through the trees. It seemed to lead nowhere, but they had no choice but to press on. They hiked and hiked, until Prue stopped and gasped.

"Check it out," she said, pointing.

The stream flowed directly into a mammoth cave entrance at the base of a tall, craggy mountain. The sisters gazed up.

"I can't even see the top," Piper breathed. The awkward, ugly mountain extended up, up, up into a swirling cloud cover.

Gazing into the cave, they saw that its mouth was constructed of boulders. The enormous rocks had been arranged in an almost perfect, graceful arch. It had clearly been built, rather than carved from nature.

"Let's go in," Phoebe said.

They stepped into the damp, dank cave. All they could see was a small, dark, unremarkable chamber. Until Phoebe touched Prue's shoulder and pointed to a back corner of the cave.

"An opening," she said. "Looks like it leads to another chamber."

They ducked through the doorway to find a second chamber—dank and dim, much like the first one. This chamber led to another, and then another. They walked steadily from room to room until Piper suddenly stopped.

"Prue, Phoebe," she whispered. "I just realized something. The light in this cave—it's not coming from behind us anymore."

"You're right," Phoebe realized, feeling a chill swish across the back of her neck.

"It's coming from *inside* the cave," Prue said.

Clutching one another's hands, they plunged into the next chamber. And there, sitting on a throne of moldering rocks, was Nikos!

His Greek god tunic had disappeared. So had his paint-daubed artsy look. Instead, he was dressed in a velvet suit, the same driftwood brown color of everything else in Hades. His floppy black curls had been slicked back severely. And he was smoking a long, foul-smelling cigar. He crossed his long legs and sneered at the sisters.

"What took you so long?" he drawled. "My, you look a fright, don't you?"

"Nikos," Phoebe said, taking a halting step toward him. "Are you all right? What . . . what's happened to you? Where are the other models?"

"I'm perfectly all right, now that I've escaped my wretched ruse up there," Nikos said, pointing upward with a curled lip. "I was a starving artist in a little white dress. My lord of darkness, into what depths I plunged to get you to my house."

Then Nikos threw back his head and laughed.

Phoebe felt a wave of nausea wash over her. She looked desperately at her sisters, who were gazing steel-faced from Nikos to her.

"Who are you?" Prue demanded darkly.

"I've already introduced myself," Nikos snapped. "My name is Nikos. Of course, I didn't give you my job title, did I?"

"No, I don't think we had a chance to exchange business cards," Piper said sarcastically. "I guess you're not really a painter."

"No, I'm a prince," Nikos said.

"Ha!" Phoebe spat.

"Prince of Hades, to be exact," Nikos continued, curling his lip at Phoebe. "Eventual ruler of the underworld, torturer of the dead, terror of the night, blah, blah, blah. Very boring job, really. My father hates it."

"Oh, my God," Phoebe whispered.

"No, not quite yet, Phoebe dear. My father's the god of the underworld for the time being," Nikos said lightly. "But maybe someday. Funny coincidence, isn't it, Prue, that you gave me the role of Hades in your stupid photo? I couldn't have engineered *that* better myself."

Phoebe couldn't believe this was happening. Of all her dates from hell, this was the ultimate.

"Where are the other models?" Prue asked, stepping threateningly toward Nikos's throne. "Did you spirit them here?"

"Heh-heh-heh," Nikos said, heaving himself off his throne and pacing in front of the sisters. "They're here all right. Perfectly safe, I assure you, although they look as disheveled as you do. They're tucked away."

Nikos flicked his hand absently in the direction of yet another cave chamber behind him. This must be an entire network of caves, Phoebe thought. Naturally, an underworld royal palace would be a damp, underground chamber.

"Why did you bring the models here?" Piper demanded.

"Why, isn't that obvious?" Nikos said. "They're hostages. They're bait. They've lured you into my web."

"Okay then, what do you want with *us?*" Prue demanded.

Nikos tossed his cigar to the floor and glared at Prue, his eyes suddenly flaring red as flaming coal.

"I want nothing with you!" he spat. "Bossy big sister. You were never supposed to be here!"

Piper lifted her hand to her mouth.

"It's Phoebe you want," she whispered. "You sent the centaur to kidnap her."

"Ah, the shy girl in the middle," Nikos said, still pacing angrily. "She's not so simple as she looks. Exactly."

Phoebe clutched her throat.

"So you're saying, you've kidnapped the models, and I'm the ransom?" she croaked.

"One soul." Nikos cackled as his eyes returned to their normal vivid blue. "That's all I need. But it couldn't be just any soul. Oh, that would never work. I needed divinity!"

"Well, you're barking up the wrong tree," Phoebe pointed out sarcastically. "I'm not really a goddess, Nikos. I just play one on TV."

"Please, I'm aware," Nikos said, looking Phoebe up and down again with a sneer. "See, that was my problem. True goddesses are in such short supply these days."

"Pity," Prue spat.

"Yes. There are consolation prizes, however," Nikos said, his features suddenly going dark and sinister. "When you don't have a goddess, a witch will do!"

With that, he grabbed Phoebe around the waist and pinned her arms to her sides. She kicked and struggled, but Nikos's grip was, natch, superhuman.

Piper waved her hands to freeze him, but nothing happened.

Nikos threw back his head and laughed.

"You think you can use your little freeze trick on me?" he bellowed. "You are nothing against me. I rule here!"

"Don't you mean Daddy rules here?" Prue taunted.

Nikos's face grew even darker, and his eyes glowed red once again.

"Damn you! Damn you to earth," he bellowed. With one arm still wrapped around the screaming Phoebe, he waved a hand in Prue and Piper's direction.

The two sisters screamed as they felt themselves fly backward through the cave's chambers. An instant later they were whirling back through the tunnel that had carried them to Hades in the first place. The chute roared around them like a bellowing monster.

Then, abruptly, the roaring stopped. Prue and Piper found themselves sitting on the Oriental rug in the living room of Halliwell Manor. Right in front of the camera. Right where they'd stood when they'd zapped themselves into Hades. Nothing had changed, not even the hands on the grandfather clock. It was as if they'd never left.

Except one thing was different.

Phoebe was gone.

CHAPTER
6

Piper lurched to her feet and gazed wildly around the living room. Part of her believed Phoebe had landed behind the couch. Or that maybe none of this had even happened, and her sister was about to pop out of the kitchen, munching on an apple.

"Phoebe?" she called hopefully.

Prue touched her sister gently on the shoulder and pointed into the sunroom. Piper spun to see that the models were still heaped on the floor and slumped on the wicker furniture, snoring away.

"It wasn't a dream," Prue said, her voice choked. "We were there. And he's got Phoebe."

"*He's* got Phoebe," Piper said, pointing at the most beautiful body in the pile of models—Nikos's earthly self, sleeping peacefully, his cheeks rosy and his curly hair flopping adorably over his fore-head.

"He looks like an angel," Prue said furiously.

74

"You'd never know he was really a devil," Piper agreed. "Get him, Prue."

Prue pointed at Nikos's sleeping body and waved her hand as violently as she could. I'll crash him into the wall so hard, every bone in his body will break, Prue thought.

But nothing happened.

Nikos lay between Hera and Ares, snoozing as peacefully as ever.

"What?" Prue blurted. She waved her arm at Nikos again. And again.

Piper ran up to him and poked at his shoulder. She shrieked. Her finger had plunged right through him.

"I guess you're not the only one who can astral project, Prue," Piper said. "The jerk's not even here. He probably knew the first thing we'd do was take revenge on his earthly form."

"So he shimmered his cowardly butt out of here," Prue said.

Piper kicked angrily at Nikos's image and stomped out of the sunroom.

"What do we do now?" she said.

"Attic!" Prue declared.

Together, the sisters rushed up the stairs to *The Book of Shadows*. Prue pounced upon their trusty book of spells and incantations.

"Let's see if there's anything on Hades in here," she said, flipping quickly through the book. "Hades . . . Hades . . . "

She desperately turned page after page. After a few minutes of futile page flipping, Piper said, "How about underworld? Or Lord of the Dead?"

"No, no, and no!" Prue wailed. "Okay, I've seen Phoebe do this. Piper, help me out here."

Prue held her trembling hands over the open *Book of Shadows*. Piper placed her hands next to hers. They'd both witnessed the moments when Phoebe had held her hands over the book and the pages had magically flipped to just the spell or potion she was looking for.

Their hands trembled in the air. They stared at the book's yellowed pages. The pages seemed to stare back—that is, they sat there, not moving.

"Concentrate," Prue ordered.

"I am," Piper said through gritted teeth. She squeezed her eyes shut.

After a minute went by with no sign of life from *The Book of Shadows,* Prue sighed and dropped her hands.

"It's no good," she complained. "Is it possible that there's nothing in here about Hades? I thought *The Book of Shadows* was infallible."

"Well, it was created by all the witches in our family line," Piper noted, pointing to one of the handwritten pages. "Maybe nobody's had to deal with the underworld yet."

"We're the first," Prue said grimly. "Forgive me if I don't have that pioneering spirit."

"I hear you," Piper said. "I hate feeling so helpless. What are we going to do?"

A few hours after Phoebe and her sisters had happened upon Nikos, Phoebe found herself locked in a dank, stone-walled room. She was gazing in a mirror—gaping in the mirror, actually. She couldn't quite believe what had just happened to her.

As soon as Nikos had banished her sisters from his lair, he'd dragged her, kicking and screaming, to another chamber of his dank, horrible cave. He'd tossed her into a room filled with dark, opulent furnishings—a four-poster bed draped with a black velvet spread, satin-covered chaises and chairs, an onyx wardrobe, a rug woven from gray, filmy stuff that resembled cobwebs, and a full-length wall mirror framed by gargoyles.

And she wasn't the only one in the room. There were four young women lounging around the room, clearly waiting for her. Each wore a skin-tight silver bodysuit and had long black curls dangling to her waist. Their skin was milky pale, and their eyes were smudged with smoky kohl. Their feet were bare.

"What, is it Goth Night at the disco, or am I in Hades?" Phoebe snapped at Nikos. "Really, Nikos, I thought you had more taste than this. So cliché!"

"Shut up!" Nikos roared. "What? You think gods and goddesses don't move with the times? I picked up this look in the Middle Ages, and I think it's marvelous. I trust you'll learn to like it, too. You'll have to."

Then he snapped his fingers at the young women. "Put her together. She's a mess!"

With that, Nikos had stomped out of the chamber. A heavy boulder magically rolled over the doorway, sealing the room shut. Phoebe stumbled to her feet and screamed with rage. She threw herself against the boulder, beating at it until her palms were throbbing with pain.

The door was completely lodged—impossible to

move. Phoebe considered giving it a kung fu kick, but decided against it. The last thing she needed on top of everything else was a broken foot. She slumped back to the floor and put her chin on her hands.

"Oooh!" Phoebe sputtered. "I don't know how I ever thought that guy was cute!"

She was glowering at the door when suddenly she remembered she wasn't alone in the room.

She turned around slowly, eyeing the totally creepy maidens. They were still sprawled on the furniture, eyeing her with bored, blank expressions. Their eyes were black and lifeless.

"Uh, hi there . . ." Phoebe said nervously.

The maidens didn't speak. Instead they slid off their perches and began to move toward her. They walked slowly, their hips undulating back and forth. Actually, Phoebe noticed, their feet barely touched the stone floor. In fact, they appeared to be slithering through the air.

Phoebe suppressed a scream and turned instinctively to the door, only to be confronted once more by the boulder sealing her in. She whirled around and scanned the walls—not a window in sight. She was stuck. Her only choice was to try to make nice.

"Um, okay, we haven't been introduced," Phoebe said nervously. "I'm . . . Phoebe."

The maidens formed a circle around her, inspecting her with their dark, reptilian eyes.

"So, um, how do you do?" Phoebe said, offering her hand. One of the maidens ducked her head to peer at Phoebe's hand.

"Okay, clearly etiquette is not your bag," Phoebe said. "That's fine with me."

The maiden sniffed at her knuckle. Then her tongue flicked out of her mouth and grazed Phoebe's hand. Her *forked* tongue.

"AAAAAAAHHHHH!" Phoebe screamed. She broke through the circle of snaky maidens and dashed across the room.

"*Hisssssssss.*"

They were undulating toward her. Phoebe had nowhere to run! With another shriek, she felt their icy hands grip her body, ripping away her filthy white Grecian gown and tearing at her hair.

"Get off me!" Phoebe screamed. "Stay away!"

But she was no match for them.

An hour later Phoebe found herself in front of the mirror. The maidens had finished their work and slithered out of the room when an attendant moved the boulder for them.

Phoebe stared at her reflection.

"I've been through the makeover from hell," she said dryly. "I'm trapped in a Cher video."

Instead of hurting her or possessing her or anything as mundane as that, the maidens had done exactly what Nikos ordered. They'd replaced her ripped dress with a long, slim, wine-colored velvet gown, cut low in the front and the back, with long, bell-shaped sleeves, and a gold cord hanging from her waist.

Her eyes had been smudged with black shadow, and her lips masked with pale makeup. And her hair had somehow been dyed from blond to black and curled into rigid, glossy ringlets, much like Nikos's own. In fact, all the snaky maidens had had the same inky curls, too.

"Egomaniac," Phoebe spat, yanking at her new hair and cursing Nikos. "Uch!"

She was just about to flop onto the bed when she heard the boulder at the door scrape to the side. Phoebe dropped into fighting stance.

This time a man entered, but he had the same blank, black eyes and flicking forked tongue as the maidens. Nikos must have a whole crew of snaky servants, Phoebe thought. She curled her lip at the grotesque creature. He seemed to stare right through her as he beckoned to her with a slithery hand to come with him.

"No way," Phoebe said, planting her feet on the floor.

The servant's tongue flicked, and he slithered quickly across the floor to grab Phoebe beneath the arms.

"Whoa!" Phoebe yelped as he lifted her off her feet with as little effort as it would have taken her to scoop a puppy into her arms. The servant skimmed out of the room, taking her with him.

"Put me down," Phoebe yelled, kicking at his cold, undulating legs. But she knew it was no use— this dude was going to take her wherever he wanted to. Phoebe felt panic rising in her throat. Of all the places to be without the Power of Three! How was she going to get out of this fix? Whatever fix it was, anyway. She still had no idea why Nikos was so intent on keeping her here. Was it just an evil whim? A power play? Father issues? What?

The servant carried her through a series of damp rock-lined hallways. Occasionally, they whizzed by chambers containing sumptuous furniture in which

Phoebe spotted more languid maidens lounging around. They also passed an enormous dining room, with a table that could probably seat forty.

For all the luxury of this underground palace, there wasn't an ounce of warmth here. The walls were damp and dark and imposing. The floors— cold, hard stone. There was little light and even less heat. Phoebe's teeth were chattering by the time the servant finally turned into one of the chambers and deposited her unceremoniously in a large carved wood chair.

Phoebe looked around. The room was filled with red velvet couches and chaises. Tables were laden with fruit, meats, cheeses and big decanters of wine. And in the middle of it all was Nikos, wearing a robe and slippers and nuzzling the neck of a snake maiden. Other maidens were fawning over him, too, giggling and flicking their forked tongues flirtatiously. Nikos took a loud slurp from a goblet of wine and grinned at one of the snake girls. She giggled shrilly and shook her long curls.

"Oh, gross," Phoebe muttered. Then she jumped to her feet.

"What's going on here, Nikos?" she demanded.

Nikos took another long sip of wine and then looked Phoebe over lazily.

"Ah, Phoebe, much better," he said. "That hairdo really suits you. Blond—not your color, darling."

"Whatever," Phoebe sputtered. "I demand to know why you've brought me here. And where are the other models?"

"Now, Phoebe," Nikos drawled, crossing his legs and popping a grape into his mouth. "I don't see how we can have a civilized conversation when you're in such a state. Sit down. Relax. Have some wine."

The moment he said the words, one of his snaky maidens shoved a brimming goblet of red wine into Phoebe's hand. She glared at Nikos. This was all a game to him! She threw the goblet to the floor, watching the thin, rose-tinted glass shatter. The wine oozed across the stone, looking scarily like blood.

"I want answers," she said, returning her gaze to Nikos, "and I want them now."

He glared at Phoebe and flicked a finger at one of the manservants guarding the door. Immediately, the servant grabbed a cloth and swept away the broken glass and spilled wine.

Nikos lurched to his feet, stumbling a bit. He's drunk, Phoebe thought.

"You really ought to be happy, you know," Nikos said. "It's not every day a girl gets spirited away to become the bride of royalty."

"The *what!*" Phoebe shrieked. "Did you just say . . . *bride?*"

Nikos sighed and rolled his eyes.

"I know," he said. "The very word makes me cringe as well." Then he shrugged his shoulders. "But there's nothing that can be done."

"Okay, wait a minute," Phoebe sputtered. "What are you talking about?"

"Sit down, Phoebe," Nikos said coldly.

Phoebe planted her hands on her hips and prepared to defy the order, but then she looked around. The door was guarded, and Nikos clearly wasn't going to attack. She might as well try to warm up.

She curled her lip at her stark, carved chair and walked over to one of the sumptuous velvet chairs. One of the snake maidens was curled within it, nibbling at a pear.

"I'll take this seat, thank you," Phoebe said archly.

The maiden hissed at her. But when Nikos shot her an irritable glance, she slithered out of the chair. Phoebe sank into the soft cushions and rubbed her chilled arms. Then she glared at Nikos and waited.

"Phoebe," Nikos said, a sarcastic grin tugging at the corners of his mouth, "I want you to marry me."

"Uh-huh," Phoebe said dryly. "I can tell. You're treating me with so much respect and affection."

"Oh, please," Nikos said, rolling his blue eyes. "As if affection and marriage have anything to do with each other."

"On earth, they do," Phoebe retorted.

"Ha," Nikos laughed dryly. "Well, in Hades, marriage is an obligation. Look at my parents."

"Spare me your psychobabble," Phoebe said. "All I want to know is why you want to marry me."

"Okay, that was an exaggeration," Nikos said, popping another grape into his mouth. "I *have* to marry you. It's a dad thing."

"Dad, meaning Hades?" Phoebe said, feeling the hairs on the back of her neck stand up.

"Yes." Nikos sighed sullenly. "My father thinks I'm irresponsible."

"Imagine that," Phoebe muttered, eyeing the boozy feast.

"He's ordered me to take a bride by my twenty-fifth birthday," Nikos continued. "If I don't, I'm banished."

"Banished where?" Phoebe asked, arching her eyebrows.

"Earth!" he replied with a sneer. "Doomed to live a humdrum life with no power, no magic, walking among mortals who, between you and me, are *not* the most attractive sorts."

"Right back at you," Phoebe spat, glaring at the blank-eyed babes slithering about.

"My father's spell has already been cast," Nikos said, ignoring Phoebe's slur. "If there's not a ring on my finger the morning of my twenty-fifth birthday, I'll instantly be sent . . . up there."

He shuddered visibly as he referred to earth.

"And as I told your sisters, I can't take just any bride," he continued, running his hand over his slicked-back curls proudly. "I'm a prince of the underworld, after all. A divine being."

"Uh-huh," Phoebe replied.

"Pity there's such a shortage of single goddesses these days," Nikos lamented. "You were the best I could come up with. I knew you were the one the minute I heard your name—Phoebe. You know, the original Phoebe was a Titan, the goddess of the moon. Face it, darling. This was meant to be."

"So all that talk at the coffeehouse . . ." Phoebe said, her steely anger faltering for a moment.

"You fell for that?" Nikos said. "Please, darling. You're not my type. I mean, you're not bad-looking . . . at least, not yet."

"What's that supposed to mean?" Phoebe demanded, jumping to her feet. A finger of fear was worming its way into her gut.

"Well, we are going to be married," Nikos said

blandly. "You'll be, you know, the old ball and chain? I'm sure it won't be too long before you let yourself go."

He snickered and pointed at one of the tables, groaning with food. It held an entire turkey and a cornucopia of vegetables; an alluringly steamy tureen of creamy soup; cakes, pies, and a tray piled high with chocolates.

"You might as well get started," Nikos sneered, getting to his feet and handing Phoebe a plate. "Eat till you're huge. I don't care. All I need is the wedding ceremony."

"Never!" Phoebe screamed, throwing the plate to the stone floor. She wanted to claw the eyes out of the bowing, scraping servant who lurched forward to sweep the china shards away.

"You're wrong, my dear," Nikos said. With three strides of his long legs, he was standing before her. He grabbed her wrist, wrenching it painfully in his strong, thin fingers. Then he reached into the pocket of his robe.

Phoebe gasped and tensed every muscle, waiting for Nikos to pull out a blade, a bludgeon, or some other kind of weapon. His eyes glowed red with rage as he thrust his hand before Phoebe's face. Clutched in his fingers was a ring.

An engagement ring. Phoebe stifled another gasp—this time of admiration. The center stone, emerald cut, was a canary diamond. It must have been six or seven carats, as garish as every stick of furniture in the grotesque castle. Still, even if it was way too showy, the glinting, gold stone was dazzling.

On either side of the diamond were large triangular rubies—as red as the spilled wine, as red as Nikos's sinister eyes.

Nikos gripped Phoebe's left hand and shoved the ring onto her fourth finger. It fit perfectly. This is too eerie, Phoebe screamed inside.

As soon as he'd wrenched the ring onto Phoebe's hand, Nikos dropped it. Then he skulked back to his perch on the couch between two fawning maidens.

"So, I've given you a gift. Now you'll have to think of something for me," he said snidely. "After all, my birthday's coming up—August fifteenth."

Phoebe put a hand to her forehead. "That's—"

"Right," Nikos said. "Five days away. Which means our blessed nuptials, Phoebe darling, are in four days."

CHAPTER 7

Piper was flopped on her favorite living room sofa, staring despondently into the sunroom.

"How can they just sleep like that?" she muttered, feeling a twinge of envy. If only she could fall asleep and forget this living nightmare. Phoebe was trapped in Hades, and she and Prue couldn't seem to find any solution.

Not that Prue wasn't still trying. She was curled up in a chair nearby, the enormous *Book of Shadows* on her lap, scanning each page carefully. Every once in a while, she shook her head irritably and flipped the page.

"Maybe we should just photograph ourselves again and go back to Hades," Piper suggested miserably. "We could try a stealth attack—just grab Phoebe and get out of there."

"I don't think that'll work," Prue said. "Remember that long trek through Hades to get to his cave? We'd be so exhausted by the time we got there, I doubt we'd be effective. Especially without our powers."

"And our powers are useless on Nikos," Piper said.

"Besides, if it were possible to sneak out and work our way back to earth," Prue pointed out, "Phoebe would be back with us by now. I just know she's stuck in that palace."

"Wondering why we haven't swooped in to rescue her, I'm sure," Piper said.

Prue was gazing back at a page in *The Book of Shadows*. She held up a finger and said, "Wait a minute. I think I may have found something."

"What is it?" Piper exclaimed, leaping to join Prue on the couch.

"Here, an incantation for lost souls," Prue said, pointing at a smudged page of text. " 'When a wandering spirit evades you, Say thee this spell, for it will aid you . . .' "

Piper shrugged at her sister. "Sounds good to me," she said.

"We don't have the Power of Three," Prue warned. "So let's say it three times, just to be sure."

Prue and Piper clasped each other's hands and read from the book.

" 'Spirit, O spirit, where are you roaming, follow our call and return to us running. Spirit, O spirit . . .' "

Three times they chanted the incantation. They clutched each other's hands so hard, their knuckles went white. At the last word, Prue and Piper opened their eyes and gazed at each other hopefully.

Piper looked wildly around the room, but Phoebe was nowhere to be seen. Piper sighed and turned to

Prue. But Prue was looking beyond her, pointing at the wall, gaping, trembling.

"What?" Piper shrieked, following Prue's gaze. Prue was staring into a small, gilt-framed mirror, one of Grams's favorite antiques. It hung on the wall next to the kitchen door.

"Oh my . . . Phoebe!" Piper cried, jumping to her feet. Prue was right behind her. Together they gazed into the mirror. Instead of their own reflections, they saw their sister, or at least a ghostly projection of her. She was pacing angrily back and forth in a small room with stone floors.

"It looks like she's locked in some sort of bedroom," Prue breathed. "See the four-poster bed? And there's a velvet chaise."

"And *what* is she wearing?" Piper gasped, pointing at Phoebe's tightly curled black hair and her flowing Gothic gown. She spotted something else, too—something shiny, yellow, and red—glinting on Phoebe's ring finger.

Prue clutched the mirror frame as the picture grew hazier and hazier, and finally disappeared entirely. In a moment Prue and Piper were left staring at their own incredulous faces.

"Well, that clinches it," Piper said. "We know that Phoebe is trapped in Nikos's castle, and she's being dressed by someone with really tacky fashion sense."

"At least she's okay," Prue said. She began pacing the living room just as Phoebe had been pacing in the vision. "But that spell is obviously useless at bringing Phoebe back to us!"

"Not to mention our other lost souls," Piper reminded her, pointing at the pile of sleeping bodies.

Prue threw her hands over her head and stomped in frustration. She glanced around the room desperately and spotted something lying on the floor next to the antique camera. It was the library book on Victorian portraiture that had given her this whole ancient Greek idea in the first place. She'd kept it nearby during the shoot to use as a reference.

Who knows, Prue thought. Maybe if I hadn't put Nikos in his element in my classical portrait, none of this would have happened.

"Ugggh," she grunted, stalking across the room. "I wish I'd never *seen* this stupid book."

She scooped it into her hands and flung it at the wall. It bounced off the plaster and landed, pages up, on the Oriental rug.

Piper picked the book up, intending to remove it from Prue's sight. She was about to slam it shut, when something caught her eye.

The book had fallen open to another classical photograph. This one portrayed one man with a full, woolly gray beard, a barrel chest, and his fists on his hips.

"Zeus, lord of Mount Olympus," the caption read.

Piper's brain started to buzz. She began adding up the puzzle pieces in her mind. Suddenly, an idea came to her.

"Of course!" she exclaimed, rushing over to Prue. "I think I know what's happening."

"You do?" Prue said, blinking.

"Did you see that ring on Phoebe's finger?"

"Yeah," Prue said. "It looked like a yellow diamond. There might have been rubies on it, too. I thought I saw a flash of red."

"A diamond ring," Piper said breathlessly. "An *engagement* ring."

"What?" Prue gasped.

"I think Nikos has kidnapped Phoebe to be his bride," Piper announced. "After all, his father, Hades, did the very same thing. He went up to earth and snatched Persephone, forcing her to become queen of the underworld."

"That's right," Prue said. "But didn't you tell me she only stays in Hades for half of each year?"

"Yes, because she ate a pomegranate seed while she was there," Piper said. "For that one morsel of food, she was doomed to spend half of eternity in Hades."

"Okay, Piper, if you're trying to give me a confidence boost, it is definitely not working," Prue scowled.

"I'm not finished," Piper said excitedly. She stabbed at the photograph in Prue's library book. "It was Zeus, the king of the heavens and lord of all the gods, who made that decree. He ordered that Persephone had to atone for that one pomegranate seed. But also that she could cut her time in Hades in half."

"So what you're saying is . . ." Prue began.

"If Zeus could do it for Persephone, maybe he could do it for Phoebe," Piper said, slamming the book shut. "Zeus is number one. He has power over his brother Hades and the underworld."

"So if we contact Zeus . . ."

"And why couldn't we? We've already been to Hades," Piper interrupted. "So we know Mount Olympus exists."

"We can ask him to decree that Phoebe be set free!" Prue said.

"All we have to do is figure out how to get up there," Piper said, grabbing *The Book of Shadows* from the couch.

"Well, that, and hope that Phoebe hasn't eaten anything in Hades," Prue said.

Piper grew pale.

"You're right," she agreed.

"And you *know* how Phoebe likes to eat," Prue added, going white herself. "She's a total grazer. She's always hungry!"

"Let's just hope," Piper said, flipping madly through *The Book of Shadows*, "that the idea of marrying the prince of Hades has killed her appetite."

Fortunately, *The Book of Shadows*, which had had no mention of Hades in it, did have a page devoted to Mount Olympus.

"I guess it's not so surprising," Piper said, peering at the page. "After all, Mount Olympus has to be a more appealing travel destination than Hades."

"I don't know if I'd call this a vacation, but you're right . . ." Prue said, leaning over Piper's shoulders. "So what do we have?"

"Potion and incantation," Piper said, jotting down the potion's ingredients. "It looks like the sun acts as a sort of portal into Mount Olympus. You can enter only during sunrise and exit at sunset."

"Okay, that's doable, I guess," Prue said. "So how do we get there?"

"Well, here's the wrinkle," Piper said, frowning at the page. "It looks like only one of us can go."

"What?" Prue protested. "Why?"

"Well, the person traveling to Mount Olympus drinks the potion. But someone on earth has to send

this person up there, and more importantly, call her
back down."

"So you're saying the person on earth, at
sunset . . ."

"Utters this incantation," Piper said, pointing to a
poem in *The Book of Shadows*. "That's what draws her
friend on Mount Olympus down through the sunset
portal."

"Okay," Prue said. "We can do this. All we have to
do is—watch out!"

"Wha—" Piper saw her sister's face contort in
horror. She ducked, just in time to feel something
zing by her cheek. Piper straightened up in her seat
and gaped at the arrow imbedded in the wall near
the living room door. She turned to see a figure, more
horrible than any of the creatures they'd seen thus
far, standing in the kitchen door. Its skin was slimy
and yellow, and its hair was, well, it wasn't hair. It
was a nest of writhing, hissing snakes.

The creature drew another arrow from a basket
hanging from its shoulder. When it looked down to
hook the arrow into its bow, Piper grabbed Prue and
yanked her behind the couch.

"What are you doing?" Prue said, trying to
wrench herself free of Piper's grip. "Let's fight it! We
can take it on."

"Not this one, Prue," Piper squeaked. "I recognize
that creature from Greek mythology. It's a Gorgon."

"I give up. What's a Gorgon?" Prue said as an
arrow zinged into the couch, neatly piercing its tap-
estry upholstery. "Darn it, this couch is an antique!"

"Forget the couch," Piper breathed. "Have you
heard of Medusa? She was a Gorgon. They're crea-

tures with snakes for hair and a lethal stare. Make eye contact with one and you'll turn to stone."

"So either we're impaled by an arrow or we're turned to stone?" Prue asked.

"Or we figure out how to vanquish it without looking at it," Piper said.

"Uch, we don't have *time* for this," Prue said, cringing as another arrow zinged into the couch. "We have to focus on saving Phoebe."

"I think that's exactly why a Gorgon has been sent into our living room," Piper said. "To prevent us from doing just that."

"Oh no," Prue groaned. Then a thought flickered across her face. "Wait a minute. The mirror!"

She pointed to the mirror in which they'd seen Phoebe's image. It hung just over their heads.

"Piper," Prue said, "Do you think you can freeze the Gorgon without looking at it?"

"No idea," Piper said. "I'll give a shot."

Squeezing her eyes shut with concentration, Piper tried to picture the Gorgon, in all its slimy, snaky ugliness. Then she lifted her hands over the back of the couch and waved them.

The grandfather clock stopped ticking. A dust mote floating by Piper's head suddenly halted in midair.

"It worked," Piper said.

Prue started to stand up, but Piper grabbed her.

"Even frozen, the Gorgon may be able to turn us to stone," she whispered. "In the myth of Perseus, Medusa's head was lethal, even after it was chopped off her body."

"I'll be careful," Prue said. "Cover me."

Keeping their eyes downcast, Prue and Piper

stood up. They could see the Gorgon's clawed feet, frozen in place on the kitchen tile. Prue crept to the wall and pulled the mirror off its hook. Then, holding the mirror in front of her eyes like a shield, she walked over to the Gorgon. Next, she placed the mirror right in front of the creature's head. She could see the snakes of its hair, frozen in midhiss around the mirror's frame.

Then Prue held her breath.

Agonizingly, the seconds ticked by, or rather didn't tick by. Then, suddenly, time unfroze. The grandfather clock chimed. The breeze outside rustled through the trees. And the Gorgon let out a horrible shriek.

With a wretched, crackling noise, its scaly feet went gray and immobile. The snakes petrified. She tapped at the Gorgon's toe with her shoe. It was pure rock.

"Prue, that was brilliant," Piper said, taking the mirror from her sister's trembling hands. "The first thing the Gorgon saw when it unfroze was its own reflection, instantly making it turn itself into stone."

Prue lowered the mirror and gazed at the Gorgon. Even as a chunk of rock, it was horrible to behold, especially with its features contorted in pain and revulsion, a moment captured from its last second of life.

"I'd suggest putting it in the garden, but it's way too ugly for a lawn ornament," Prue said wryly.

"And it must weigh a ton," Piper complained, leaning on the horrible sculpture. "How are we ever going to get it out of here?"

"We'll deal with that later," Prue said. "Right now, let's focus on whipping up that potion. At sunrise tomorrow morning, one of us has to head to Mount Olympus."

An hour later Prue and Piper were in the kitchen, peering at the potion recipe.

"Okay, I think we've gathered up all our ingredients," Prue said. "Lavender stems, thyme, sage, and saffron . . ."

"It *would* have to be a whole tablespoon of saffron," Piper complained. "It's only the most expensive spice ever. And I was planning on making paella next week!"

"*Anyway,*" Prue said, glaring at Piper, "we've also got our red clay, rose thorns, and ugh, scales from a silver fish?"

"Glad I have that salmon in the freezer," Piper said.

"And last but not least, stone chipped from a sculpture."

"What a coincidence," Piper said, grinning at Prue. She opened the cabinet beneath the kitchen sink and burrowed into the toolbox the sisters stored there. She emerged with a hammer and chisel. Then she stalked over to the Gorgon statue, which was still standing— totally in the way—in the kitchen doorway.

Ching!

With one swift whack, Piper whacked one of the stone snakes off the Gorgon's head. She tossed it across the room to Prue with a cackle.

"Revenge is sweet," she said. "Okay, what's next in the recipe?"

"Now we just simmer all this stuff for four hours," Prue said, squinting at the recipe, "in a base of red wine, water, and . . . song?"

"Hmmm," Piper said. Then she winked at her sister and pulled a boom box out of the china hutch.

"A portable CD player," she said, "is a chef's best friend."

Piper sifted through a stack of CDs and popped a Green Day disk into the boom box. Then she plugged it in, hit Play, and placed the stereo next to the stove.

"Thank goodness for auto-replay," Prue said.

As Piper began measuring and mixing the ingredients in a saucepan, Prue bit her lip.

"You know, we haven't discussed the most important part," she said. "As in, which one of us is going up to Mount Olympus?"

"Well, I just assumed you would," Piper said. "You know, you being the oldest with the most active powers and all. I'll just stay at home . . . as usual."

"Actually," Prue said, "I was thinking just the opposite. You'd be a much greater asset up there negotiating with Zeus."

"Yeah?" Piper said. She gave a small smile and laid her measuring spoons on the counter. "Why do you say that?"

"Well, there's your incredible knowledge of Greek mythology, for one," Prue said. "I mean, I always thought you were a geek in high school. Who knew one day all that knowledge would be the thing to save our family?"

"Uh, thanks," Piper said, rolling her eyes.

"It's also probably a good idea for me to stay here in case any other creatures from Hades pop up,"

Prue said, wiggling her telekinetic fingers. "I can zap them before they try to harm our sleeping beauties in there."

"Good call," Piper said, resuming her measuring. "So it's settled then. I'll go up to Mount Olympus."

As she said it, she felt a thrill shoot through her. She'd always imagined what Mount Olympus must be like when she was a kid, studying mythology in school. It had been a fun fantasy, like wondering what it would be like to fly like Mary Poppins or go back in time like Ebenezer Scrooge.

Now she couldn't believe she was actually going to *go* to Mount Olympus. As worried as she was about Phoebe, she also couldn't wait to venture to the heavens.

"Do you know what this means, Prue?" Piper suddenly said. "Tomorrow I'll be in heaven and Phoebe will be in hell!"

Prue couldn't help but snort.

"Oh, I shouldn't laugh," she gasped, "but there is some poetic justice in this, don't you think?"

"Hee, hee!" Piper giggled. Then a sound made her gulp back her laughter.

The doorbell! Piper shot Prue a panicked look.

"Who's at the door?" Prue squeaked.

"And what if they see our models?" Piper squeaked back. "Here, you go draw the curtain and guard the babes with your life. I'll go get rid of whoever is at the door."

"Check," Prue said. Both sisters ran out of the kitchen. Piper watched Prue zip the curtain across the brass rod, hiding the sunroom—and the sleeping heap of models—inside.

"Madelaine's snoring again," Prue whispered. "Whoever it is, don't let them inside!"

Piper nodded, gulped, and headed into the foyer. Putting on an expression that said, "It's six o'clock, and don't you know civilized people are eating dinner," she swung the door open.

"Mitchell!" she blurted.

There was Prue's adorable new potential boyfriend, standing on the front porch. Piper couldn't help noticing how cute his compact, muscular body looked in a French blue shirt and perfectly fitting Levi's.

Piper heard a gasp from the living room. Prue must have heard her. Piper knew now was the time to get rid of Mitchell, but something made her hesitate.

"Um, hi," she said, trying to smile normally. "You must have a date with Prue."

"Yup," he replied, shuffling his feet on the porch. He's waiting for me to invite him in, Piper thought. What do I do?

"I managed to get Prue to commit to dinner right before she shoved me out the door yesterday," Mitchell said with a self-deprecating laugh. "I hope the rest of the shoot went all right?"

"Oh yeah," Piper said. "It was great! Just . . . dandy. Mitchell . . . can you hold on for a second? I don't think Prue's ready yet. Why don't you sit on the porch and enjoy the fresh air. I'll be right back."

Piper whisked the door shut and scurried back into the living room. Prue was clutching at the velvet sunroom curtain. Her other hand was clapped over her mouth.

"I totally forgot I told Mitchell I'd go out with him tonight," Prue gasped. "I'll just have to tell him I can't go."

Piper could see Prue's eyes filling with regret. Prue sighed.

"I guess that'll be it then," she said. "What guy's going to tolerate me blowing him off two days in a row? Another relationship killed by the Wiccan life."

Prue gave another deep sigh and headed for the front door. But Piper held up her hand.

"Wait," she said. "You know what? We're paralyzed until sunrise anyway. There's nothing we can do until I can get to Mount Olympus. And I can handle the potion—I am a chef, after all. Why don't you just go?"

"Are you kidding?" Prue said. "Phoebe's in mortal danger and I'm supposed to go on a date?"

"Hello?" Piper said. "That is a great guy out there. You don't want to lose him. And, in case you haven't noticed, it seems like we're in mortal danger every week. It'll keep. Just have dinner with him, if only to make sure he'll ask you out again. I'm giving you a sisterly order."

"Well, I guess all I'd be doing is sitting here and stewing," Prue said, biting her lip. "Are you sure you don't need my help with the potion?"

"It's cake," Piper said. "Easier than paella, that's for sure."

"Well . . . okay," Prue said, perking up. She rushed for the stairs. "I'm going to go throw myself together. Tell him I'll be five minutes. And Piper?"

"Yup?"

"Thank you—you're the best."

"You betcha," Piper said with a wink, feeling both happy for Prue and a little wistful. When's the last time a guy had shown up on the front porch, pining away for her? With a sigh, Piper went to the kitchen, where she poured Mitchell a cold drink. Then she headed to the front porch.

When she opened the door, Mitchell was sitting on the top step. He glanced over his shoulder at the sound of the door, his eyes filled with hope. His shoulders slumped when he saw that she wasn't Prue.

"She's late, as usual," Piper said, trying not to giggle at the outlandishness of the lie. "Five minutes is all she needs."

"Oh, great," Mitchell said, a smile lighting up his face. "For a minute there, I thought Prue was going to brush me off again."

"Not a chance," Piper said, smiling down at him. Then she held out the frosty glass in her hand. "Lemonade?"

CHAPTER 8

Mitchell pulled his SUV up to a curb on a cobblestone-clad little street in downtown San Francisco.

"I hope you don't mind," he said, jumping out of the vehicle to open Prue's door for her. "I made a reservation for us at this trattoria. I'm practically a regular here. After our Vietnamese adventure, I thought maybe we should try something closer to home."

Prue slid out of the SUV and straightened her dress—a pumpkin-colored satin shift with a plunging backline. Then she looked up at the small, quaint sign.

"Rose of Napoli," she read. Crusty bread, she thought. Pasta in red sauce with lots of Parmesan cheese. Chianti. In other words—comfort food. Exactly what she needed. She flashed a smile at Mitchell. "It's like you read my mind."

"Perfect," he said, shooting her one of his adorable grins.

As they sat down at a small corner table, Prue couldn't help but think of Phoebe. Her sister was in a place that couldn't be more different from this cozy restaurant. Even the thought of dinner made Prue feel guilty, as she remembered the curse that eating could mean to her sister.

When Mitchell ordered a bottle of red wine and poured her a glass, Prue eagerly took a swallow. Anything to distract her from the anxiety gnawing in her belly.

A bowl of penne primavera and two oversize glasses of wine later, Prue was feeling much more relaxed. In fact, she found herself laughing out loud at Mitchell's story of his first journalism job.

"So, the editor asked me, 'Where did you see this scene in your lead? It's fantastic,' " he was telling Prue. "And I said, 'Exactly. I made it up.' "

"You what?" Prue gasped, putting a hand over her mouth as she giggled loudly.

"I was such a rookie, I had no idea that you couldn't, say, pose a hypothetical," Mitchell said. "So, she takes me aside and says, 'This is journalism. You *can't* make things up!' "

"I can just see you, all young and earnest and . . . making things up!" Prue said, bursting into more giggles.

"Yeah, laugh if you will," Mitchell said. "I almost ended my career before it began."

"Well, you seem to have recovered nicely," Prue said. "I mean, *National Geographic*. It's the pinnacle of adventure journalism. Tell me what it's like, working for them."

"How about I tell you over dessert?" Mitchell

said, signaling their waiter for the check. "I know just the place . . . "

Half an hour later, Prue found herself staring up at the stars. She turned to Mitchell and smiled. Then she shifted to get into a more comfortable position on the hood of his SUV. They were parked high on a bluff over the Pacific Ocean, lying back on the windshield and gazing into the night sky.

"This is my favorite place for dessert," Mitchell said with a shy smile. Then he sat up and peeked into the to-go box from Rose of Napoli.

"Cannoli or tiramisu?" he asked.

"Definitely tiramisu," Prue said with mock seriousness. Mitchell handed her the creamy dessert and a plastic fork. Prue took a bite and groaned.

"This is the best tiramisu I've ever had!" she exclaimed.

"Take a taste of this," Mitchell offered, holding out the cannoli. "You'll think you died and went to Sicily."

Prue laughed and took a bite of the crunchy dessert.

"Oh my God, you weren't kidding," she said, laughing. Then she shook her head in amazement. "I'm having such a nice time with you. It's hard to believe that—"

Prue stopped herself abruptly. She'd felt so comfortable with Mitchell, she'd almost spilled the beans about Phoebe. Which, of course, would reveal to Mitchell that she was a witch. Which would, of course, kill any chance she had of a relationship with him. Prue's smile melted away and she glanced down at her hands.

While she was brooding, Mitchell slipped off the hood of the SUV. A minute later he reappeared in front of the truck, holding a camera. Prue was startled out of her reverie. She blinked at Mitchell.

"What are you doing?" she asked, suddenly feeling uncomfortable.

"You just looked so beautiful sitting there, staring at the stars," Mitchell said, looking sheepish. "And then I remembered I had my camera in the trunk."

"Oh," Prue said. She shook her head. What's the big deal, so he wants to snap your picture, she tried to tell herself. But something inside her was squirming.

"I . . . I don't think I want to be photographed," Prue said, ducking her head. "I'm sure I look a mess. It's breezy up here."

"Oh, are you one of those photographers who can dish it out but can't take it?" Mitchell teased. He lifted his camera to his eye. "C'mon, just one snap."

"Don't," Prue said. She tried to sound jovial, but she was fighting down a bubble of panic rising within her. Her face felt hot and there was a buzzing in her ears.

"Smile. Please, Prue," Mitchell said insistently, holding the camera before his face.

"No!" Prue said, sliding off the SUV abruptly. I can't do this anymore, she thought to herself. My sister's life hangs in the balance and I'm having a romantic moment under the stars? What kind of a horrible person am I? Home—gotta get home.

"I-I'm sorry," Prue stuttered, cringing at the shock on Mitchell's face. She slumped against the truck and quickly thought up a lie. "I'm . . . I'm really stressed about my work right now. And when you pulled out that camera, it all came flooding back."

"Oh, man," Mitchell said, walking over to Prue and hooking the camera over his shoulder by its strap. "I've ruined everything. I wanted to take you away from your work worries, not remind you of them."

Mitchell wrapped his strong arms around Prue in a gentle hug. She bit her lip, feeling a stab of guilt about her lie. Although, if she thought about it, she *was* stressed about her work. It just wasn't the profession that Mitchell knew about.

"Listen, what can I do to make you forget your troubles?" Mitchell asked.

"I'm sorry," Prue replied. "But you know what? There's nothing either of us can do. I had such a great time tonight, but now I think I'd better get home."

"Of course," Mitchell said. "I understand."

But he didn't move. His hands rested warmly on the back of her neck. He began massaging her tense muscles. And, despite herself, Prue felt herself leaning into him.

Mitchell's hands moved down her back, softly touching her bare skin. Prue sighed very quietly. And before she knew it, Mitchell's lips were covering hers in a soft, warm kiss. Before Prue could stop herself, she was sinking deeply into the kiss, wrapping her arms around his neck.

Mitchell was kissing her neck, her earlobes and then her lips again. His kisses were more passionate, more insistent. Prue responded, kiss for kiss. And suddenly, she didn't want to go home anymore. She wanted to stay here under the stars, with Mitchell, forever.

He pulled away for a moment and touched the tip of her nose with his, gazing deeply into her eyes.

"Oh, Prue," he whispered. "I'm in heaven."

Heaven . . . Mount Olympus . . . It all came flooding back. What's wrong with me? Prue thought suddenly. Here I was, all ready to go home and deal, and one kiss later, I'm flaking out on my sisters.

"I've . . . I've gotta go," Prue replied regretfully.

Mitchell breathed deeply, regretfully, and nodded. Then he opened up the SUV for Prue and helped her into it.

In a short while, they were parked in front of her house.

"Mitchell, I'm sorry if I sent you mixed signals tonight," Prue said, reaching up to smooth back his soft brown hair. "I . . . I really did have a wonderful time. It's just that I have stuff I need to take care of."

"Well, do you think you'll find relief enough in your busy schedule to go out with me again?" he asked, gazing at her with his huge gray-green eyes.

"Oh yes," she replied. "I mean . . . I hope. I mean, I'll call you, okay?"

Mitchell looked deep into Prue's eyes, as if he was trying to read her sincerity. She wished she could be less cagey. Planting one more quick kiss on his soft lips, she quickly opened the car door and trotted up the front walk. She turned and waved before she stepped through the front door.

Once inside, Prue leaned against the front door and tried to sort out her thoughts. For some reason, she felt just as anxious about making things work with Mitchell as she did about rescuing Phoebe. She shook her head—what *was* wrong with her? She barely knew Mitchell. And nothing was more important than getting her sister back safe.

"It must be all that Chianti I had at dinner," Prue said, shaking her head again. She stalked to the kitchen, eyeing the bottle of potion, corked and ready, on the counter.

After pouring herself a big glass of water, Prue popped a couple of aspirin and went to her room. She set her alarm clock for 4:30 A.M.—a half hour before sunrise—and flopped into bed. Almost immediately, she fell into a fitful slumber.

The next morning Piper slumped into the kitchen while it was still dark out. She was dressed in leggings and a soft, comfortable cotton top. She was tying on running shoes when Prue came into the kitchen.

"Planning for an athletic event up there?" Prue said, cocking a puffy eye at Piper's getup.

"Who knows, after Hades," Piper said, rolling her eyes. "I just want to be ready for anything."

"Smart move," Prue said. "Me, I'm ready for coffee."

"Made you a whole pot," Piper said, pointing to the coffee machine in the corner. "You've got a long day of waiting ahead of you."

"Yeah, well that's nothing compared to what's in store for you," Prue said worriedly. "Are you ready?"

"I'm excited actually," Piper admitted. "Mount Olympus! Not many mortals ever get the chance to see the likes of this."

"Well, get ready to grab that chance," Prue said, squinting out the kitchen window. "Because I can see the first hint of light. I'd say sunrise is about five minutes away."

"Wow," Piper said, peering out the window with her sister. "I can't remember the last time I was awake for the sunrise."

"I think it was Christmas morning, 1979," Prue joked.

Piper had to laugh. Then she gave Prue a quick hug. "We can do this," she whispered. "Don't worry."

"I know," Prue said, blinking a tear away. She handed Piper the potion and grabbed the incantation she'd copied from *The Book of Shadows.*

"Ready?"

"Ready," Piper said, taking a deep breath.

Prue squinted at the paper in her hand and began to read.

" 'To the heavens, take this traveler, As the sun rises, the sky shall have her. One day she'll walk among the clouds. Protect her with heaven's benevolent shroud.' "

As Prue read, Piper uncorked the potion. She held her nose and slugged it back in two big swallows.

Then Prue stared in amazement as Piper began to fade from view. Piper stared back and gave a little wave. Then she dissolved into a shaft of light that shot through the ceiling and disappeared.

Prue stumbled out onto the back porch and looked into the sky, which was just turning pink with the first rays of the sun.

"Good luck, Piper," she whispered. Then she went inside for the long wait.

Piper gasped as she felt herself becoming corporeal once again. She wasn't sure where she'd gone

when she shimmered out of the kitchen, or how long
she'd been traveling. But as she watched her hands
graduate from wispy apparitions to solid wiggling
fingers, she knew—or at least hoped—she'd arrived
on Mount Olympus.

Quickly, she gazed around her. Then she blinked.
Okay, *this* wasn't what I expected, she thought.
Clouds, winged creatures, and lots of Corinthian
columns, maybe. But this? What is this?

She was standing—scratch that, she was *floating*—
in a sort of swirling silver bubble. The walls looked
as if they were made of mercury. Even stranger, the
bubble felt warm and soft and enveloping, though it
looked cold and metallic.

Piper looked down and gasped again. Her prag-
matic leggings and running shoes had been
replaced by a sleek body suit with the same silvery
cast as her surroundings. She took a tentative step,
even though her feet seemed to have nothing to
grip onto. But somehow, she felt herself moving
through the bubble.

"Okay, we have movement," Piper whispered.
"The question is, where am I moving to? Whoa!"

Suddenly, Piper felt the bubble open beneath her,
stretching into a long, narrow tunnel. She plummeted into the hole, and with nothing to grab onto,
felt herself sliding through the chute at warp speed.

"Aaaaahhhh!" Piper screamed. And then, to her
surprise, she started laughing wildly. Because . . . this
was fun! After the initial shock of her fall, she realized she felt as if she was whizzing through a warm,
totally thrilling waterslide. She almost didn't want
the wild ride to end.

But of course, it did. Piper found herself ejected from the tunnel and deposited into a new room. Instead of a mercurylike bubble, this room was wispy, cottony, not quite there. Piper got to her feet and looked around.

"Welcome."

Piper jumped and spun around. But she saw no one. The room, or whatever she was standing in, was empty.

"Hello?" she called nervously.

"You are Piper Halliwell," the voice said. It was a woman's voice, soothing and mellifluous, almost musical.

"Okay, this is giving me the creeps," Piper muttered. Not only because this voice knew her name, but because she felt as if the voice was speaking from inside her own head.

"Don't be afraid," the woman said.

For some reason, Piper was able to obey. She relaxed. She let her guard down. She felt safe.

"Um," she began, "I'm here to—"

"See Zeus," the voice finished for her.

"Well, yes!" Piper exclaimed. "You see, I—"

"Have a sister who is in danger," the voice continued. "No need to continue. I can read your mind."

"Oh," Piper said, feeling the creeps reenter her system. She pulled at the tight neck of her silver bodysuit nervously.

"Your clothing makes you uncomfortable," the voice said. "No problem. You don't need it any longer. You passed the first test and emerged from the antechamber."

"Test?" Piper asked the air. "What do you mean?" Then she gasped as her silver bodysuit disappeared and was replaced, not by her original outfit, but by a long filmy gown, as warm and supple as anything she'd ever worn. The dress was the most beautiful, shimmery pale blue.

"Not just anybody can make it into Mount Olympus," the voice said. "Surely you know that."

"Well, that makes sense," Piper said. "But how did I pass the test? I didn't do anything."

"Purity of spirit," the voice said. "Honesty. True need. We scanned you for them."

"*Scanned* me?" Piper said. "Okay, this is starting to sound like a bad Arnold Schwarzenegger movie. What next?"

"More tests," the voice said. "You will walk through a series of portals. Should you be judged worthy, you will see Zeus."

"Ohhh," Piper said nervously.

"Do not be afraid," the voice said again. "Just keep walking."

Piper took a deep breath and did as the voice told her. She walked and found herself squelching through the wall of the wispy chamber. It was even warmer and softer than her beautiful dress. The next thing she knew, she was in a room filled with water. At first Piper panicked and spun around to get back to where she had come from. She opened her mouth to scream. But that's when she realized, she could breathe. She was breathing water.

Grinning with delight, Piper swam through the chamber, doing a few somersaults and deep dives before she found herself sucked into the next chamber. This room had opalescent walls and was filled with soft shafts of pastel-colored light. Piper sighed with delight and found herself wondering if she could recreate such an effect at P3.

Next, another portal yawned open beneath her. Piper dropped through it and let herself slide through a tunnel. This trip was shorter and calmer, but the landing—the landing was out of this world.

Because waiting for her at the bottom of the tunnel was an enormous man. He must have been seven feet tall, with an imposing build. His broad shoulders were draped with a long, soft, pale gray robe. The man's hair was the same beautiful gray color as his garment, and it draped across down his back in soft waves.

"Zeus," Piper whispered. This had to be him. He too, was not what she'd expected. All the sculptures and paintings she'd seen depicted a mischievous, tunic-clad, bearded patriarch. Instead, this man felt both comforting and frightening, as powerful a being as Piper had ever seen.

"Indeed," Zeus said to Piper. "Come with me."

In a blink, Piper found herself seated in front of the god in a room that was all white. Mist swirled around them, and beyond the mist, Piper could make out a circle of attendants, young men and women in gowns and tunics much like her own. She sat on a shapeless but incredibly comfortable cushion, just like Zeus's.

"Tell me," Zeus said simply, placing an enormous hand on each of his knees.

Quickly and tactfully (after all, Nikos was technically Zeus's nephew), Piper explained everything that had happened from the moment Nikos brought his magical camera into their house.

"I'm afraid that Nikos wants to marry my sister, just the way Hades married Persephone," Piper said. "But please, Zeus, we're witches destined to protect innocents. And without the Power of Three, we're useless."

"You know our history?" Zeus asked quietly.

"Yes."

"So you know what doomed Persephone?"

"Eating a pomegranate seed," Piper answered.

"Has your sister taken any food in Hades?" Zeus quizzed.

"I don't know," Piper said, growing more tense.

Zeus clapped his hands on his knees.

"Your trial is this," he announced. "At dark they come without being summoned. By light they are lost, without being stolen."

Piper felt a moment of panic. She knew this scenario—it pervaded Greek mythology. A mortal asking a favor of the gods would be asked an impossible riddle. If the mortal was clever enough to come up with the answer, his wish would be granted. Now it was Piper's turn. Her entire family depended upon her cleverness.

She closed her eyes and thought about Zeus's cryptic words. Dark, they come. Light, they go. Dark . . . night . . . sky . . . Piper's eyes flew open.

"The stars!" she exclaimed. "You've described the stars in the night sky!"

After Piper blurted her answer, Zeus sat still in his seat. There was a long, long pause. And then he clapped his hands.

"Your sister is free!" he announced. "As long as no morsel of food has passed her lips."

"Oh, thank you," Piper said, jumping to her feet. "Will you spirit her out of Hades or—"

"Oh, I cannot invade my brother's domain," Zeus said, holding up his hands. "You must go and find your sister and bring her back. All I can promise is that the creatures of Hades will not impede her escape."

"Oh . . ." Piper said, dejected. Part of her wondered why she'd gone to the trouble of consulting Zeus, but she tried to stifle the thought, knowing the Olympians could read her mind.

Too late.

"My dear, I realize this doesn't solve all your problems," Zeus said, glowering at Piper. "But believe me, without the protection of my decree, your sister would *never* make it out of Hades. If you can get to her before Nikos brings her to the marriage altar, and before she eats a bite of food, she will be protected by my power on her journey from Hades."

"I understand," Piper said, clasping her hands in front of her. "I can't thank you enough."

"Good-bye," Zeus said abruptly, returning to his cushion.

"May I ask one more question," Piper said. "What about our models? Are they under your protection as well?"

"For them, my dear," Zeus said dryly, "you are on your own. Only the Power of Three is my concern."

With that, Zeus clapped his hands and a quartet of attendants leaped forward to escort Piper out of the room. Before she had a chance to utter another word, she was squelched out of the chamber through yet another portal and sent on her journey back to earth.

"Well, I guess this is a case of take-what-you-can-get," Piper muttered as she floated back through the brilliantly lit chamber. "Hang in there, Phoebs. I'm coming!"

CHAPTER
9

After Piper shimmered away, Prue looked around the kitchen, feeling more helpless than she'd ever felt. Prue had always been the go-getter in the family, the leader who got things done. But now, she was at home holding down the fort while her sisters fought battles in "points beyond." There wasn't even any housework she could do because Piper had cleaned up so thoroughly after making the potion the night before. The kitchen was sparkling.

Prue walked into the living room and took a peek behind the velvet curtain into the sunroom. She curled her lip at the sleeping models, who looked as rosy-cheeked and beautiful as ever.

"How do they do it?" Prue wondered, glancing in the wall mirror at her own puffy, sleepy eyes and tangled hair. "You'd think twenty-four hours of sleep would take its toll."

She was sick of looking at the models, especially

the apparition of that creep Nikos. Prue was just about to yank the curtain shut again when she spotted the old Victorian camera, which stood just as she'd left it after the previous disastrous photo shoot.

"Hmm, might as well see what ended up on the film plate," Prue murmured dully. It was hard to imagine how important the 415 cover had seemed to her just yesterday. Now she could barely bring herself to care.

"All it takes is a little kidnapping to put things in perspective," Prue said dryly. She grabbed the metal canister in which she'd stored the glass negative plate and ambled down to her darkroom in the basement. "Anyway, processing this film will keep me busy."

In the hazy light of the darkroom's red bulb Prue prepared her chemicals and then transferred the image from the delicate glass plate to photographic paper. Then she gingerly started to process the photograph.

As the photo began to bleed to life in the developing fluid, Prue held her breath. Finally, the balance of light and color was perfect and she transferred the photo to a tray of fixative solution. She added a little sepia toner to the final wash to give the picture an antique finish, and finally the picture was complete.

Prue snatched the undulating square of paper out of the bath and flicked on the overhead light. Squinting in the glare, she inspected the image.

Her eyes flew first to Nikos.

"This photo is bound to show his true colors," Prue muttered, cringing to think at how badly the gorgeous guy had duped them all.

Gazing at the curly-haired man with his arms

draped over her sister's shoulders, Prue had to admit it. There was no way to tell that Nikos was the prince of Hades. In fact, he looked cute.

Prue scowled and turned her attention to the rest of the photo. She held it at a distance and gazed at it as a whole. Then she gave a little gasp. Her image was perfect. Every one of the eight models, even Piper, looked serene and beautiful. The light flooding the sunroom was natural and golden. The composition was balanced, yet completely original.

This is incredible! Prue thought, slapping a hand on her forehead. The first and only shot. And somehow I came up with this? Maybe that camera is magic in more ways that one!

Shaking her head in amazement, Prue climbed the stairs. She had no more work to do in the darkroom, so she might as well find something else to do upstairs. After taking another peek at the models— still gorgeous and healthy—and patrolling the house for mythological creatures, she looked at her watch.

"It's only nine!" she wailed. "Sunset is hours away. I'm gonna go mad."

"I'm gonna go mad if I have to spend one more night here," Phoebe muttered through gritted teeth. She was slumped on an overstuffed couch in her windowless room, bored stiff and hopping mad. All morning the snake maidens had been slithering in, wielding trays of food. But each time, Phoebe barred their path or chased them out of the room. The last one had left just a few minutes earlier.

"Stay away from me!" Phoebe had shouted, grabbing a tray of lamb chops and mashed potatoes out of the maiden's hand and throwing it to the hallway floor. The woman had narrowed her eyes and hissed at her, then skittered swiftly away.

Phoebe clutched her growling stomach. She was actually dying to eat something. But the thought of those snake maidens preparing her food, their forked tongues flickering over it, nauseated her. She shivered and rubbed her arms.

"Oh, Prue, Piper," she whispered, "Where are you?"

Scrrrrrrrrrraaape.

Phoebe whirled around. The boulder at her doorway was moving aside again. How *do* they do that? she thought with frustration. She got ready to scream at yet another snake maiden invading her personal space. But instead she gasped.

Standing in the doorway was a young woman— no forked tongue, no black, reptilian eyes. In fact, but for the goofy Goth costume that matched Phoebe's own, this girl could have been a classmate of hers at college. She held a basket of food—fruit, cheeses, a dish of caviar, a baguette, some pâté. A classic French picnic.

"Who are you?" Phoebe demanded.

The woman stepped inside the room and the boulder slid into place behind her, locking them in together.

"Hi," the woman said, extending her hand. "I'm Jessica."

Phoebe didn't return the handshake. Instead, she sat up on the couch and gazed at the woman in confusion.

"Are you a prisoner, too?" Phoebe asked.

Jessica threw her head back and laughed, her long dark curls bouncing.

"No way," she said, sliding seductively into a chair near Phoebe. She placed the basket at her feet and began laying the food on the coffee table between them. "I choose to live in Hades."

"Oh, really?" Phoebe said. Then a stricken look crossed her face and she lifted her hand to her mouth. "Oh, are you . . . are you dead?"

Jessica laughed again and shook her head.

"Okay, let me get this straight," Phoebe said, crossing her arms, "you didn't get here by being buried with one obol, or whatever, and you weren't snatched. You're just here on vacation? What, you couldn't get a hotel room in the Caribbean?"

"Phoebe, you're fighting it," Jessica said, evading Phoebe's questions. "You're here now. Embrace it."

"I don't follow you," Phoebe said. Suddenly, she spotted a ring on Jessica's finger almost exactly like hers, with emeralds instead of rubies. Stacked against it was a diamond-studded wedding band.

"Wait a minute," Phoebe blurted. "Are you—"

"Married to the mob?" Jessica giggled. "Yup. Nikos's older brother, Philip. He's just as gorgeous as Nikos. Wait till you meet him."

"What, at my bridal shower?" Phoebe scoffed sarcastically. She was appalled to see Jessica nodding enthusiastically.

"We're all so excited that you've arrived," the young bride said. "Me and my sisters-in-law. There are eleven of us. Nikos is the youngest, the last to marry."

"Oh my God," Phoebe breathed. "So you're telling

me you were all kidnapped to become brides, just like me?"

"That's such an ugly word," Jessica said, spreading a little caviar on a cracker and biting into it with a luxurious smile. "Mmmm. Want some?"

She held a spoonful of the glistening caviar out to Phoebe, who was eyeing the gourmet food hungrily. But she shook her head. She had to focus. This woman had clearly been brainwashed or something. She didn't want to succumb to the same spell.

"Please," Phoebe said. "Tell me what happened to you."

"I've been married to Philip for one wonderful year now," Jessica said.

"No," Phoebe said urgently, "I mean, how did you come to be Philip's wife?"

"I embraced it," Jessica said dreamily. "Phoebe, you have no idea . . . you don't know how fun it will be."

"Fun?" Phoebe gasped.

"If you embrace it," Jessica said, nibbling on some pâté, "it's like one long party."

"What's 'it'?" Phoebe sputtered. "What do you mean?"

"Mmmm, this pâté!" Jessica exclaimed, her eyes wide. "Phoebe, you've got to try it. Have you ever had pâté?"

"Please, my sister is a chef," Phoebe spat. "I've had plenty of pâté."

"I take it you don't like the food the maidens have been bringing you?" Jessica said. She leaned forward and giggled again. "Between you and me—they kind of creep me out, too! That's why I prepared this little picnic for us myself."

Jessica dragged a strawberry through a silver dish of whipped cream and took a bite.

"Mmmm," she said. "So yummy. You've got to try one."

"I think you'd better leave my room," Phoebe said coldly.

Jessica cast her eyes down, looking hurt. "I thought we could be friends," she said. "It would make your transition easier, you know."

"There isn't going to be any transition, Jessica!" Phoebe yelled. "Leave! Now!"

Jessica glared at Phoebe and tossed her strawberry stem over her shoulder with a snotty scowl.

"Suit yourself," she said, flouncing toward the door. The boulder magically slid aside. As she prepared to step outside, Jessica turned and glared at Phoebe. "But you'd better eat something. You've got a long few days ahead of you. You know, wedding preparations and all."

"Out!" Phoebe screamed. Jessica yelped and hurried away. Then the boulder rolled back, sealing Phoebe's chamber closed.

"Ugh!" Phoebe growled, flopping back down on the couch. "Talk about in-laws from hell!"

She tried for about the zillionth time to wrench the enormous engagement ring off her finger, but it remained tightly in place. She almost screamed with frustration. She couldn't understand what Jessica could like about Hades, about being a captive bride with nothing to do but lie around all day, eating gourmet treats.

Gourmet treats which seemed to be taunting Phoebe. For all the food that Jessica had eaten, the coffee table was still groaning. In fact, it was laden with Phoebe's favorites. Caviar, strawberries, chocolate . . . the feast couldn't look more succulent.

Another hunger pang wrenched Phoebe's stomach. She eyed the doorway warily. She believed Jessica when she'd told her the slimy snake maidens hadn't touched this food. And it certainly smelled good. Phoebe licked her lips and scanned the spread hungrily. Then she grabbed the caviar spoon.

But as soon as she touched it, a tremor racked her body and an image—one of her premonitions—spilled into her mind. She saw Jessica! Jessica crying and wailing and beating on a boulder door, just like hers. And then . . . the young woman was sitting in a bed, a four-poster bed, looking white and wan. Someone was feeding her morsels of food. She chewed listlessly, her eyes vacant and shadowed. And then another vision popped into Phoebe's head. Jessica was dancing in a parlor with another glossy-haired young woman. A cluster of gorgeous men with piercing blue eyes glanced at them from the periphery, stifling yawns.

Phoebe lurched out of her dream state with a gasp. The caviar spoon fell from her hand and clattered onto the stone floor.

As usual, the premonition was cloaked in mystery. All she could be sure of was that the food Jessica had eaten had appeared to transform her from a sullen, desperate prisoner, much like Phoebe herself, into a happy-go-lucky party girl.

Phoebe clutched her throat and stared at the feast. All day long everybody here had been urging her to eat, parading trays of tempting treats before her.

Something about this food was dangerous—she was sure of it.

Wailing with anger and hunger, Phoebe slapped at the silver dish with the back of her hand. She watched it fly across the room, spraying the wall with sweet, snowy whipped cream. The dish clattered to the floor as Phoebe flounced onto the bed, burying her head in her pillow.

"Now, this really is my worst nightmare," she whispered. "I never thought I'd see the day when I, Phoebe Halliwell, master of the pig-out, snacker extraordinaire, would go on a hunger strike."

Piper had made her way back through the series of chambers—the opalescent room with the mesmerizing lights, the water-filled chamber, the wispy, cottony nest. She'd been sucked upward through the water-slide tunnel, and now she was back in the mercurylike antechamber.

She was also back in her silver bodysuit, which meant her watch was gone, gone to wherever the rest of her clothes had disappeared to. Piper floated idly in the bubble, wondering how long she'd been in Mount Olympus.

She gazed around her, still enraptured by her swirly, silver surroundings. Mount Olympus is more magical and more otherworldly than anything I could have imagined. I can't believe I actually saw it.

Then she frowned.

"I just hope my day here was worth it," she whispered to herself. "I hope we can get to Phoebe in time. Hey, speaking of which . . ."

Piper looked around her excitedly. The light in the

antechamber was changing. When she'd entered, the chamber had been bright and shimmery. Now it was darkening, and the bottom of the bubble was glowing orange.

"This must be sunset!" Piper exclaimed excitedly. She couldn't believe the day had gone by so quickly. She must have entered a kind of time warp when she came to Mount Olympus. She held herself still and closed her eyes, getting ready to make the journey back to earth. Any minute now, she thought, Prue will say the incantation and zap me back home.

Prue plodded down the stairs of Halliwell Manor and glanced at the grandfather clock. Six o'clock. She had at least another hour until sunset. She sighed. She'd already organized her negatives, dusted the entire house, taken a long, refreshing bath, and vanquished one more demon from Hades—*another* pesky Gorgon! Pretty soon, boredom was going to reduce her to starting her Christmas cards, five months early.

"Well, that's something to do," she muttered as the doorbell chimed. "Get rid of whoever's at the door."

Prue smoothed the old tank top and shorts she'd thrown on and opened the front door.

"Mitchell!" she gasped.

"Hi, Prue," Mitchell said, offering her an armful of creamy pink tulips. "I hope you don't mind my dropping in like this. I just . . . well, I had to see you again. You're all I've thought about since I dropped you off last night. I know you're busy, but I thought I could offer you a little break?"

"Um, well . . . " Prue said, swiping a hand through

her hair. Not only was she in a totally awkward position here, but she looked a mess. This was so going to blow it with Mitchell.

"At least let me come in and help you put these in some water," Mitchell said, raising his eyebrows at Prue.

"Oh, of course," Prue stuttered. "I'm sorry. Come on in."

Peeking into the living room to make sure the sunroom curtain was closed, Prue motioned Mitchell into the kitchen. She pulled out a vase and ran some water into it.

"Do you have any pennies?" Mitchell asked.

"What?" Prue blurted, looking at Mitchell as if he was crazy.

"Pennies," Mitchell repeated. "You put pennies in the water and they make the tulips open up."

"Okay, I'm not even going to ask you where you learned that," Prue said, laughing and reaching for the jar on the desk where she and her sisters always tossed their change.

"I told you, it's an occupational hazard," Mitchell said. "With every story, you pick up weird little bits of trivia. This I learned covering the Chelsea flower market in New York."

"You're sure you didn't learn it from an old girlfriend?" Prue said, cocking an eyebrow as she dug a handful of pennies out of the jar.

"Positive," Mitchell said. "Here, I'll take those."

As Prue handed the coins to Mitchell, their fingers touched. It was like an electric shock.

"Whoa," Prue said. Then she clamped her lips shut. Had she actually said that out loud?

"I know," Mitchell replied, his grin fading and his beautiful eyes going soulful. "I felt that, too."

"Mitchell," Prue began, "I ca—"

Mitchell stopped her by placing a finger on her lips. Prue felt another jolt of attraction shimmy through her. And before she knew it, she'd kissed him.

Mitchell cradled her face in his hands and kissed her back, passionately. Prue leaned against the kitchen counter and wrapped her arms around his neck. Her eyes slid closed. Mitchell's kisses were overwhelming. They wrapped her in warmth. They made her forget everything.

The orange glow coursing through the silvery bubble seemed to have reached its peak. Piper was mesmerized. She couldn't believe how beautiful the sunset was from this vantage point.

She lost herself in the vivid color and the swirling silvery atmosphere of this womblike place. She thought again about what a magical day she'd had. Then suddenly, a realization broke her reverie.

The orange glow. It was fading. Piper felt panic well up in her throat.

"Prue . . . " she murmured. "Where are you?" The light was growing dimmer with each passing minute.

"Oh no," Piper said, whirling around in alarm. She saw no portal. No escape from this bubble, which was beginning to feel more claustrophobic with each breath she took.

Piper closed her eyes. Breathe, she told herself. Just breathe. Prue is the most responsible woman on earth, and she's your big sister. She will not fail you. Sunset isn't over yet.

Piper felt her panic subsiding. She kept her eyes closed and clasped her hands in front of her, expectant that at any moment, she would feel her body grow lighter and finally shimmer away. Then she'd be zapped back into her nice, cozy kitchen.

Piper breathed deeply, feeling thankful for those yoga techniques Phoebe had taught her a few weeks ago.

But in the back of her mind, a little voice was saying, Forget the yoga! Something's gone horribly wrong!

Piper released her calming breath in a gust and let her eyes flap open. Her worst fear had been realized. The antechamber was black. The sun had set—minutes ago!

Which meant Piper was trapped in Mount Olympus for twenty-four more hours!

"Prue!" Piper yelled into the abyss. Then she began to sob. "Where are you?"

Prue wrapped her arms more tightly around Mitchell's slim waist. She kissed him deeply, her eyes clamped shut. Her mind felt blissfully empty of everything except the warmth of those wonderful kisses.

But suddenly, something gave her a jolt. It sounded like a voice, a panicked shout, in fact, in the back of her mind. Prue's eyes flew open. And what she saw made her gasp. She pulled away from Mitchell's still-puckered lips with a shriek.

"Oh, my God," she cried.

"What?" Mitchell gasped. "Prue, are you all right?"

Prue trembled and pointed through the kitchen window. Mitchell whirled around.

"What? I don't see anything," he said, puzzled.

Exactly. That was the problem. It was dark out.

Prue had become so immersed in making out with Mitchell that she'd completely forgotten about both of her sisters. She'd missed the sunset. Piper was trapped on Mount Olympus. Which meant Phoebe was still trapped in Hades. Prue had lost them an entire crucial day. She had ruined everything.

Prue was so stunned by this horrible realization that she was almost hyperventilating. She shoved Mitchell away and spun around, clutching the edge of the kitchen counter.

Think, she told herself. There's got to be some way of fixing this. Think.

"Prue," Mitchell said behind her, his voice worried and sympathetic. "What is it?"

Prue just shook her head and waved Mitchell away, her back still turned to him.

"I . . . I just remembered something," she choked out. "You have to leave, Mitchell. I'm sorry, but you have to leave right now."

"I don't think so," Mitchell replied. Prue cocked her head. Had she heard him correctly? Mitchell's sweet, mellow voice seemed to have become so chilly, so threatening.

"Besides, Prue," he continued, his voice getting even deeper and colder. "It's too late. There's nothing you can do to save your sister now."

Prue spun around. Then she screamed. Mitchell's

beautiful, chiseled face was contorting. His skin was darkening to a sickly green color. His lips were blackening and curling back to reveal growing fangs—yellow and dripping with saliva. His shoulders were growing broader and sloping downward, splitting the seams of his soft gray T-shirt. He grew taller and taller.

In an instant Mitchell had transformed into a beast more horrible than any of the demons that had invaded Halliwell Manor over the past day. He loomed over Prue, gripping her shoulders with his claws. His breath, hot and acrid, felt like it was burning her face.

Prue squirmed, trying to wrench herself from his grip. Tears squeezed out of the corners of her eyes as she tried to wrap her brain around the horrible truth, the truth that Mitchell—or the monster he had become—voiced for her.

"Without the Power of Three, you'll never be able to save Phoebe," he grunted. "Your bond has been broken Prue. And all for a kiss. Distracting you was ridiculously easy. My lord Nikos will be so pleased."

CHAPTER 10

No!" Prue screamed.

The monster—who only minutes earlier had been sweet Mitchell, the best kisser on earth—threw back his green, scaly head and laughed.

"Oh, yes," he said in a thick, guttural bellow. His claws tightened on Prue's bare shoulders. "You have forsaken your sisters, Prue."

"Not . . . possible," Prue wept. "How . . . "

"Oh, think about it," the monster said sarcastically.

Prue did. She remembered the first time she'd met Mitchell at the library. He'd been so charming and he'd . . . he'd handed her the book. The library book on Victorian portraiture. He'd led her straight to the portal to Hades!

Prue shuddered at the realization. Mitchell had volunteered to assist her at the photo shoot. Nikos must have wanted him on hand to back him up if things didn't go according to plan—if Prue hadn't done his dirty work by photographing everyone with his cursed camera!

Suddenly, Prue realized something else.

"You were trying to send *me* to Hades, too," she spat at Mitchell's repulsive face. "When you tried to photograph me last night. That's why you were so insistent."

"Right again," the creature said. "How did you get so smart all of a sudden? But when you wouldn't cooperate by looking into the lens, I had to come here to intercept you in another way. Hope you enjoyed it . . . *Prue*."

Mitchell curled his monstrous green face into a smirk and licked his cracked, blackened lips.

Prue screamed with rage. Even though her arms were pinned to her sides by Mitchell's gruesome claws, she managed to flick her hands toward him. She focused every telekinetic power in her possession on the horrible creature. Her anger helped to propel him, bellowing, across the kitchen. He landed on the kitchen table. The legs splintered and collapsed beneath his weight.

This only enraged Prue more. She was sick of having to replace furniture after demons stormed into the house. This place was falling apart!

"Argh!" Prue screamed, waving her arm at Mitchell again. He flew off the demolished table and crashed into the beadboard wall, making a splintery dent in that, too. Prue shook her head and ran across the kitchen, leaping at Mitchell and crashing the sole of her foot into his jaw.

"Aaaahhhh!" the creature bellowed. He lashed

out with his fist and caught Prue in the cheek, sending a spasm of pain shooting through her face. She
sprawled backward onto the floor but quickly
sprang to her feet. Mitchell was whirling his tail—his
tail!—over his head. It spun so fast, Prue could hear
it making a whizzing sound. Then the long spike-
tipped limb shot out at Prue as fast as a frog's
tongue. She jumped to avoid it, but the tail caught
her ankles, sending more pain jolting into her body.
She crashed onto the counter.

Grimacing, Prue realized how badly she needed
her sisters right now. With Piper's power to freeze
time and Phoebe's superior kung fu—not to mention
the Power of Three—the sisters together could vanquish just about anything. But, at this moment, all
alone, Prue was seriously doubting her ability to conquer monstrous Mitchell.

Clutching her throbbing ankle, Prue scrambled off
the counter and crouched behind it, trying to catch
her breath.

"Scared, are you?" Mitchell growled, stomping
across the kitchen floor. Prue could hear that lethal
tail of his whizzing through the air again. She
focused on her power and stood up, howling with
vengeance. Then she waved her hand at Mitchell's
tail. Her force caught the limb in midswing and
wrapped it around Mitchell's own neck.

The monster gaped with surprise and emitted a
sickly, choking noise. Prue zapped him with another
wave of telekinesis, pulling his tail tighter. He pawed
at the limb with his razor claws, and Prue almost
laughed at the grimace of pain that crossed his
ghastly features. To save his own neck, he's going to

have to cut off his own tail, Prue thought with satisfaction.

"Who's scared now . . . *Mitchell?*" she shouted,
waving her arm again. This time the tail pulled
Mitchell toward the kitchen door. He stumbled
weakly and attempted to flail his claws at Prue. She
just cackled and gave him another telekinetic blow.
Mitchell's tail dragged him into the living room. By
now his lurid green scales had gone a bit paler and
Mitchell's breath was raspy. He was struggling to
stay conscious. Yeah? Good! Prue thought, waving
her hand once more.

Then she dashed around the monster to yank back
the velvet curtain hiding the heap of models in the
sunroom. Mitchell's tail continued to yank him
along, until finally, Prue relented. Mitchell stood
before her, swaying and gasping for air. His head
swung over his sunken green chest.

"Oh, Mitchell," Prue called sweetly. She saw his
yellow eyes roll up to glance at her. She ducked
beneath the black drape on the back of Nikos's
cursed camera and quickly adjusted the lens so the
monster was in her frame.

"Say Hades," she yelled. Then she popped the
shutter.

Mitchell threw back his head and roared. As the
shutter closed, his bones seemed to turn to rubber
and he collapsed under his own massive weight. He
fell directly backward, right on top of Nikos's apparition. With a poof of smoke, Nikos's beautiful image
disappeared. An instant later Mitchell's horrible
specter shimmered away, as well.

Prue ran into the sunroom to make sure Mitchell

hadn't injured any of the sleeping models with his fall. But no, they were all fine.

Prue stood up and took a deep breath. The demon was out of the way. But that had been the easy part. Now she had to figure out how to remedy her horrible mistake.

Prue rushed into the living room and began pacing back and forth. Okay, she thought, surely there's a way out of this. But how? She knew *The Book of Shadows* would be no help. After all, it had already given her instructions for spiriting Piper back from Mount Olympus. And she'd flubbed the simple requirement—that she utter the incantation at sunset.

How hard would it have been to do it right? Prue berated herself. After all, she'd been lying around all day, focused on performing one simple task. And then, when the crucial moment came, she'd totally dropped the ball!

Prue stopped pacing. Suddenly she realized Mitchell's kisses must have carried some sort of spell, some magic that would compel her to forget her responsibilities, indeed, *everything*. That's why she'd been so intoxicated by them, why she'd abandoned ship every time she and Mitchell locked lips.

Prue shook her head. Still, that's no excuse, she raged inwardly. She had messed up bigtime, and Prue Halliwell just didn't mess up. Especially not when it came to something this big. She *had* to come up with a solution.

At that thought, Prue's mind seemed to go completely blank. She was paralyzed by the enormity of this predicament. She didn't have a clue what to do, and she was all alone. She flopped back into a chair and stared blankly at the grandfather clock, watching its pendulum move back and forth, back and forth, ticking away crucial seconds.

Suddenly, Prue gasped. She leaped to her feet and ran over to the clock. She gave it a little hug and then dashed up the stairs to the attic.

"Of course," she muttered. "The time travel spell that Phoebe wrote! We've used it to go hundreds of years back in time, why not an hour? Now I just have to find where she wrote it down."

Prue peered into the disheveled cabinet that Phoebe used to store the spells she'd written. Phoebe had also tossed in random potion ingredients and bottles, a journal of demons they'd vanquished, and what's this—some stuffed animals from Phoebe's childhood? Prue sighed with frustration and began to sift through the most disorganized Halliwell's stuff. She began pulling out scraps of paper and even a few napkins scrawled with Phoebe's handwriting. Prue sifted through the crumpled papers.

"Okay, we've got a love spell," Prue muttered, "an incantation to contact the dead, another love spell, *another* love spell—Phoebe!"

Prue rolled her eyes and continued to rummage through the scraps of paper. She was just tossing one over her shoulder when she saw that it had something scribbled on its back. She flipped it over and sighed with relief.

"Time travel—backward," Prue read with a little laugh. "Oh, and here's time travel forward, too. Better make sure to read the right one."

She glanced over the lines and stuffed the scrap of

paper into her shorts pocket. Then she took a deep breath and began to chant.

"The bond which was not to be done, Give me the power to see it undone, And turn back time to whence it was begun."

After saying the words for a third time, Prue opened her eyes and looked at her watch. It hadn't moved! She jumped to her feet and ran to the stained-glass window at the attic's far wall. It was still dark. Phoebe's spell had worked before—why not now?

With a sinking feeling, Prue realized why: the Power of Three. She gave a dry laugh. Oh, the irony. She couldn't save her sisters . . . without her sisters!

Prue clapped a hand to her forehead and looked up at the ceiling. She couldn't believe it. She felt another tear squeeze out of her eye.

"Oh, Piper," she moaned. "I'm sorry."

She let her hand fall to her side. It landed on something soft and fuzzy. She gazed at the floor next to her and saw a worn stuffed puppy. Prue smiled slightly. She remembered that old thing—Phoebe had dragged it with her everywhere when she was a toddler. She'd called it Charles.

Wait a minute! Prue put a finger to her chin. She didn't have Piper and Phoebe with her, but she did have Charles. What if she could find things that had a true connection to her sisters. Maybe those things would harbor a bit of their spirits—and their powers.

Prue dashed down the attic stairs and into Piper's room. She looked around, deep in thought. What was Piper's most precious possession? Suddenly, she snapped her fingers—Grams's necklace.

Prue ran to Piper's jewelry box and found the delicate gold necklace and pendant—a Wiccan sun and moon—nestled lovingly in a velvet box. Grams had given it to Piper just before she'd died.

As for Phoebe's precious object . . . well, she had gone to the trouble of storing Charles in the cabinet of valuable spells and potions. And she'd spent every moment hugging that thing throughout her formative years. Charles was perfect.

Clutching Piper's necklace, Prue ran back to the attic. She clasped the delicate chain around her neck. She scooped up Charles and hugged the stuffed animal fiercely. And then she squeezed her eyes shut and recited the incantation again. Once, twice, three times.

Suddenly, Prue felt a gust of wind hit her, sending her hair flying over her head. Just as suddenly, the breeze disappeared. Prue opened her eyes hopefully and twisted around to peek at the attic window.

Shafts of sunlight were spilling through the stained glass. Prue looked at her watch: 6:45. Yes! It was about fifteen minutes before sunset.

Almost sobbing with relief, Prue ran back down the stairs and grabbed the Mount Olympus incantation from the kitchen desk. Then she hurried onto the back porch for a perfect view of the rapidly sinking sun.

Her heart fluttered in her chest as she squinted at the sun. She could see it touching the bottom of the horizon, turning a beautiful flame orange as it did. Prue waited a minute longer until the sun was half submerged.

Now!

With a shaking hand, she squinted at the incantation.

" 'From the heavens, bring the traveler,' " she read. " 'As the sun sets, the sky shall no more have her. One day she walked among the clouds. Now cast her from heaven's benevolent shroud.' "

Prue held her breath. And waited.

Then something made her spin around and peer through the window of the kitchen door. Just as she did, she saw Piper shimmer into the kitchen, standing in the exact spot from which she'd left and looking just as she had that morning, in her leggings and sneakers. She was even waving, just as she'd been when she'd shimmered away.

Prue burst into the kitchen, grinning wildly. As Piper became completely corporeal, she shook her head and looked around the kitchen, frowning at the demolished table. Then she looked down at her outfit and gave a little smile. And finally, she glanced up at Prue.

"Piper," Prue gasped. "I'm so glad to see you."

"Oh, really," Piper said accusingly. "Where were you? Sunset came and went without an incantation. But then, um, well, it came again."

"I did a time-travel spell after I missed the first sunset," Prue explained, giving Piper a quick hug.

"What was so important that I was almost stranded in Mount Olympus?" Piper demanded, scowling at her sister. "And, hey! Why are you wearing my necklace?"

Prue knew Piper was totally annoyed with her, but she could only laugh happily.

"Long story," she said. "I'll tell you later. First, tell me what you got from Zeus."

"Well," Piper said, leaning on the kitchen counter, "Mount Olympus was the most amazing experience I've ever had. These strange chambers filled with silvery swirls and colorful lights and . . . oh! You can breathe water there."

"And? And?" Prue demanded. "Did you get to meet Zeus?"

"I did," Piper said. "And, well, it's not the best solution in the world. But . . ."

"What did he say?" Prue asked.

"He said he will shield Phoebe from the demons of Hades and help her out of the underworld," Piper offered.

"And the bad news?" Prue prompted.

"Well, he's not just going to zap her back to us," Piper said with a deep breath. "We have to go get her."

Prue thought of another long, slogging journey through horrible Hades and felt her heart sink. But an instant later she was ready for the trip. After all, what choice did they have?

"Camera," she said curtly. "Let's go."

"You got it," Piper said, following Prue into the sunroom. They positioned themselves in front of the old camera and Prue grabbed the shutter release cord.

"I almost forgot," Prue said, nodding at the sleeping models. "What about our lovely friends here. Are they protected by Zeus, too?"

"Um, well," Piper said, wringing her hands.

"Piper. . . ."

"For them, he said we're on our own."

"Great," Prue said. "Just great. So we have to

snatch Phoebe from Nikos's clutches, somehow find the models, who could be anywhere in Nikos's palace, and get them all back to earth safely?"

"That sounds about right," Piper said, biting her lip and gazing at Prue with large, frightened eyes. "Do you think we can do it?"

"We have to," Prue announced with gritted teeth. Quickly, she uttered the spell that enabled them to be spirited to Hades. She was just about to push the shutter button when Piper shouted, "Wait!"

"What?" Prue exclaimed.

Piper reached around Prue's neck to unclasp Grams's necklace. Then she looked around frantically and grabbed an antique, but not heirloom, letter opener off a console in the living room. The beautiful silver-plated blade was studded with semiprecious stones. She snatched an old mother-of-pearl inkwell, too.

"Fare for Charon, the ferryman on the River Acheron," she explained to her sister, tucking the letter opener into the waistband of her leggings. She handed the inkwell to Prue to put into her shorts pocket.

"Might as well bring something with less sentimental value than that necklace."

"Good thinking," Prue said. Then she grabbed Piper's hand and clicked the shutter button.

CHAPTER 11

Down in Hades, the hours crept by. Phoebe had no idea how long she'd been in her cell, since there were no clocks or windows. And who knew if there was normal time—morning, afternoon and night—in Hades? Phoebe had a hunch that the place was mired in a perpetual twilight—a hazy, gray gloom like the kind she'd seen in the forest. The idea of spending another day here made her despair. The thought of spending a lifetime here? Well, it wasn't something Phoebe could even allow to enter her mind.

Curled up on her bed, she moaned and wrapped her arms around her stomach. It was starting to feel concave after so much time without food. Then she flailed her head, and those hateful black curls, around in frustration. There wasn't even anything to distract her in here. No books, no pictures, nothing but food.

Phoebe heaved herself off the mattress and stalked to the doorway. She pressed her ear to its edge, where the enormous boulder was nestled, locking her in. Maybe she would be able to hear snatches of conversation.

But Phoebe heard nothing but dead silence. She slid down the wall next to the door and curled up on the floor, dropping her forehead to her knees. As she fiddled with the wretched ring on her finger, Phoebe's thoughts turned to the models. She wondered where they were. Once Nikos had used them to lure Phoebe and her sisters to Hades, had their usefulness expired? Had he cast them out, to wander through the underworld, lost, bewildered, and losing valuable beauty sleep?

Or had Nikos kept them here for his amusement? She shuddered to think what Chloe would do if Nikos dyed her hair black and curled it into these stiff ringlets.

I wonder if they have Evian for her? Phoebe thought, a grim giggle escaping her lips. Then she shook the laugh away. There was nothing funny about what she'd done. She'd hired these models and brought the treacherous Nikos into her home. Now five souls might be lost, perhaps forever, because of her.

Or who knows, Phoebe thought, propping her cheek on her fist. Maybe once he got me, Nikos returned the models to earth and they're lounging around our sunroom right now, eating Piper's canapés and comparing beauty products.

She rolled her eyes at the idea. Fat chance. She didn't know this demonic Nikos well, but she could read him enough to see that compassion was not his strong suit.

Just as Phoebe was working herself up into a

major anxiety attack, she heard the now familiar scraping sound of the boulder moving aside. She stayed where she was, sullenly curled up on the floor next to the entrance. Probably just another snake maiden, Phoebe thought, slithering in to taunt me with more delicious grub.

And right she was. The maiden undulated through the doorway and headed to the coffee table without looking around the room. Phoebe tensed— the maiden hadn't noticed her crouched next to the door. She glanced at the bed where she'd spent most of the day napping and sulking. The thick velvet quilt was bunched up in a pile—a pile that looked a lot like a human body.

A realization shot through Phoebe's mind like an electric spark. The snake thinks that pile of blankets on the bed is me, she thought.

She glanced at the maiden. The servant kept her back to Phoebe as she cleared Jessica's picnic from the coffee table and began unloading her own tray. She was oblivious.

Phoebe held her breath.

Then she crept silently out the door.

Prue and Piper felt themselves shimmer into their bodies. They looked around. Sunlight blinded them, and they were rocking, rocking, hearing water slap gently against wood.

"Uh-oh," Piper said,

"Where are we?" Prue asked. "This isn't the Hades we know and hate."

"We're in a boat!" Piper blurted. Prue rolled her eyes and turned to her sister.

"I can see that," she said dryly. She and Piper were sitting in a rough, bare rowboat, about ten feet long, with nothing in it but the two planks on which they sat and two primitively carved oars. They were surrounded by water—beautiful, Caribbean-blue water.

Not too far away—maybe a mile—Prue could see an island covered in steep mountains and lush tropical foliage. The island was edged by a beautiful white beach. The boat was pointed directly at a lagoon in the middle of the beach. The clear, bright blue circle of water was separated from the sea by a stretch of sand with a small opening in it.

"This is definitely not the River Acheron!" Piper wailed.

"Was there anything in your studies about a sort of back door to Hades?" Prue said.

"Not that I can remember," Piper replied, her brow furrowed in thought.

"Well, we might as well row to shore," Prue said, pointing to the lagoon. "Let's just hope when we get there, we find some pathway to Hades."

Each sister grabbed an oar and started paddling toward the island. As stressed as they were, the steady lapping sound of the ocean waves and the warmth of the sun were soothing. Piper found herself lifting her face to the sky, soaking in the rays as she paddled.

Prue gazed at the land before them, straining to see something besides tropical trees and pristine empty beaches—a house, a structure, anything that they could go to for information about where they were.

But she saw nothing. Except . . .

"Piper," Prue said, squinting at the finger of land that enclosed the lagoon. "Did you see that?"

"What?" Piper said, peering over Prue's shoulder.

"I thought I saw something move," Prue said. Suddenly she pointed. "There! On those rocks near the lagoon entrance. I saw something flash in the sun! Something alive."

"Really?" Piper asked nervously. "I wonder what it is."

"Well, based on the company we've been keeping lately, it could be anything," Prue said grimly. "And it's probably not friendly."

"Should we sail around the island and dock somewhere else?" Piper asked.

Prue bit her lip and then shook her head.

"Let's get a bit closer to see if we can get a better look," she said. "The lagoon seems to be the easiest way into the island. If we avoid it, we'll have to climb over all those mountains."

"And time is of the essence," Piper agreed. They started paddling with more strength.

"Get ready to freeze if you have to," Prue whispered as they approached the shore. Some boulders were coming into view at the lagoon entrance. But she couldn't see any creatures.

"Maybe whatever you saw is hiding," Piper hissed.

"Or maybe it was just my imagination," Prue said hopefully.

Just then Piper saw two eyes pop above one of the boulders and stare at them intently.

"Uh . . . I don't think it was your imagination,

Prue," she said, pointing at the boulder with a trembling finger. "Someone's watching us."

Prue spotted the spy. It looked like . . . a woman! In fact, she could see a ragged mop of driftwood-colored curls above two beady, black eyes. The woman was blinking passively at Prue and Piper.

An instant later she hopped on top of the boulder.

"No way!" Piper gasped.

"Are those . . . wings?" Prue whispered.

"Wings, feathers, webbed feet," Piper whispered back. "The whole shebang."

They were staring at a creature with a woman's head and a seagull's body. The creature's feathers were white, and her legs were bright orange. As she hopped sideways across the boulder, Piper could see that her beady eyes and her head's jerky movements were unmistakably avian. This bird-woman was less grotesque than the scaly Harpy that had invaded their living room, but she was no less disconcerting.

"Head of a woman, body of a bird," Piper murmured. "Living by the sea . . . I'm sure I know what this creature is, but I can't place it."

As Piper struggled to recall her classics studies, two other bird-women came into view. With a flutter of their massive white wings, they alighted on the boulder next to the leader. Their mops of hair were sand-colored. The matted curls twitched as they angled their heads to gaze at the sisters. Their tiny black eyes blinked at Prue and Piper curiously but not malevolently.

"Okay, well, they're not attacking us," Prue whispered. "That's a good sign, right?"

"I'd guess so," Piper said. But she had an uneasy

feeling about these creatures. She pressed a palm to her forehead. Think, she urged herself. Head of a woman, body of a bird . . .

The leader opened her mouth, as if she wanted to say something.

That's when it hit Piper.

She grabbed Prue's arm.

"I know what they are!" she gasped. "Sirens! Don't listen to the so—"

But before she could finish her sentence, a bright, clear melody surged out of the creature's mouth. The sound hit Piper like a wave of pleasure. It was the most beautiful music she'd ever heard, though it had no lyrics and no melody. It enveloped her like the warmest embrace, the softest touch, she'd ever felt. And suddenly her warning to Prue, her fears, Phoebe's dire straits, all melted away.

As if in a haze, she turned to look at Prue. Her sister had a rapturous expression on her face that told Piper the music was hitting her the same way.

Next, the two other Sirens joined in. One pulled a golden lyre—much like the small harp that Prue had used in her photo—from beneath one wing and began strumming it with her feathers. The third produced a flute. Holding it to her lips with her wingtips, she played a harmony whose beauty was almost too much for Piper to bear. Yet she had to hear more.

Together Prue and Piper paddled to the shore and pulled their boat onto the beach. They climbed out of the craft and walked slowly toward the Sirens. The song grew louder and, if it were possible, even more lovely.

The sisters climbed onto the boulders and sat, staring rapturously at the creatures.

I hope the song never stops, Piper thought dimly. I want it to go on forever.

The beauty was so great, Piper had to close her eyes and lie down, the better to focus on the gorgeous music. Hazily, she glimpsed Prue do the same. Piper felt as limp as a rag doll. All the tension had left her body. All she felt was pure contentment.

Phoebe tiptoed through a series of hallways. Almost as soon as she'd left her room, she'd gotten lost, which was fine. If she never saw that stifling cell again, it would be too soon. All she wanted to do was find the models and then take the closest emergency exit out of Nikos's horrible palace.

She turned corner after corner, skulking along the damp, cold, bare walls. After a while, the floor began to slope downward. Then it became more sinuous, twisting and turning every few feet.

Every once in a while, Phoebe came upon an open doorway. Stealthily, she peeked into one room after another, seeing empty bed chambers, empty banquet halls, empty sitting rooms. Where *was* everyone in this enormous place anyway? Phoebe wondered. And how would she ever find her way out?

She shook the terrifying thought out of her head and tried to focus on the models. If Nikos wanted to hide them away, where would he put them? Hmmmm.

Suddenly, Phoebe gasped and looked down at the sloped floor beneath her feet. Of course—the dungeon.

"Not that this entire place doesn't feel like a dungeon," Phoebe muttered dryly. She looked about to make sure no slimy servants or royal family members were lurking about. Then she lifted the heavy skirt of her velvet gown and started to run.

She flew down the hallway, careening around corners and skidding on the slick stone floor. She couldn't fight the urgency and panic swelling in her gut, so she ran faster. Finally, the sloping floor evened out. And, Phoebe realized, the hallway had grown much more narrow. It was lit with flickering torches mounted on the walls. And between the torches, Phoebe saw boulders blocking doorway after doorway.

These were prison cells, much like her own.

"I guess those who aren't royal fiancées don't get the choice digs that I had," Phoebe whispered. She felt another stab of guilt as she wondered if the models were trapped in one of these rooms.

"Chloe?" she called softly. She looked around fearfully. Then she steeled her shoulders. She might be a mile beneath the royal family's living quarters. Nobody was going to hear her down here.

"Chloe!" she shouted. "Madelaine? Kurt? Are you down here?"

She paused. Then her breath caught in her throat. What was that sound? It sounded so distant, like a baby's weak, thin wails.

"Chloe!" she screamed. "Madelaine!"

She pressed an ear to one of the boulders. She heard it distinctly this time. A muffled scream.

"Heeeelllp us!"

"Oh, my God," Phoebe cried. "It's Phoebe. I'm here! I'll get you out of there, I promise!"

Then she slumped against the cold wall and whispered, "But how?"

"Good question, Phoebe."

Phoebe gasped and whirled around, shrieking as Nikos finished shimmering into the hallway before her. He was glaring at her with a curled lip. His eyes glowed red with rage.

"I went personally to your chamber to fetch you," Nikos spat. "My father is throwing a banquet in your honor, a little prewedding festivity. My entire family is there, along with all the courtiers and maidens."

Whoops, Phoebe thought, that must have been where everybody was.

"Imagine my embarrassment," Nikos raged.

"Imagine the pain of these people that you've imprisoned!" Phoebe said back to him, pointing at the cell where she was sure the models were trapped. "You've lured me here. You don't need them anymore. Please, please, can't you spirit them back to earth?"

"Don't be naive, Phoebe," Nikos said. "And don't say another word to me. I've clothed you in beautiful gowns, had food prepared for you, fixed your awful hair, and this is how you repay me? By sneaking around? What? Were you trying to escape?"

Phoebe scowled. Nikos threw back his head and cackled.

"That won't happen any sooner than you'll pry my ring from your finger," he growled. "I'd toss you in one of these cells right now if my family weren't still waiting for your appearance at this fete. We're going there now. And tomorrow morning we'll be married."

"Tomorrow!" Phoebe cried. "But your birthday isn't for . . ."

"Three days," Nikos said. "But your stubbornness requires me to resort to extreme action. Once we are wed, you are mine. Escape is impossible. Not unless the almighty Zeus interferes, a feat that is equally impossible."

Nikos cackled again and grabbed Phoebe's arm, digging his nails painfully into her flesh. She screamed as she felt herself shimmer into nothingness.

When she became corporeal again, Nikos was still clutching her arm. They were standing in a large foyer just outside the huge dining room she'd seen when she first arrived here. Festive voices, the clink of silver on china, and laughter swelled out of the room.

"We're going in. Do not embarrass me again," Nikos threatened with a sneer, "or I'll stage the wedding ceremony right now!"

CHAPTER 12

Prue had no idea how long she and Piper had been lying there, luxuriating in the Sirens' beautiful music. All she knew was that she wanted the singing to go on and on.

Yet suddenly the lovely sound stopped. Prue stirred slightly, frowning. She wanted the music back. She needed it. She heard Piper moaning softly. Clearly, she felt the same way Prue did.

Please, please, Prue begged inwardly. Play for us some more. Nothing can make me happy, ever again, except that song.

But the music didn't come. Prue groaned. Slowly, with great effort, she opened her eyes. She squinted at the bird-women. They were staring at her and at Piper. The creatures' mouths were clamped shut. And their beady, black eyes were suddenly venomous. The lead Siren, the brown-haired one, looked most hostile of all. Hopping nimbly on her orange webbed feet, she moved quickly down the boulder toward Prue. And in her agile wing feathers she was holding a knife!

Prue tried to scream, but the song seemed to have left her in an intoxicated state. She could barely lift her head, much less gather up the energy to scream. She groaned some more and struggled to move. Had . . . to warn . . . Piper . . . .

The Siren was coming closer. Twitching grotesquely, she raised the knife over her head.

Panic flared inside Prue's head, but she could still barely move. The most she could manage to do was fling her arm out.

She hoped that would be enough.

Trying as mightily as she could to focus her telekinetic powers, Prue flicked her hand weakly at the Siren.

It worked. A surge of energy shoved the evil creature back, tumbling her off the boulder and into the surf. Prue heard her scream in rage. This sound was as piercing, as grating, and as terrifying as the Siren's song had been beautiful. It pierced Prue's brain like a lightning bolt and cleared it of some of its fog. She blinked hard and looked at Piper. Her sister was clutching her ears and lurching weakly to her feet.

"Prue," Piper rasped. "These Sirens . . . lure sailors to their death with their hypnotizing song. They're going to kill us!"

"Not if I can help it," Prue declared, stumbling to her feet as well. She waved her arm and sent Siren #2 tumbling into the ocean. But by then the angry leader had flown back onto the boulders with a violent flap of her wings. She was still clutching her knife, and she was bearing down on them fast.

"Piper!" Prue yelled.

Piper nodded and waved her arms at the advancing Siren. Instantly, she froze in space, her face caught in a hideous grimace. The third Siren froze, too.

"Run!" Prue said.

Though still weak, the sisters managed to clamber down from the boulders. They began stumbling down the beach, heading to the thick canopy of tropical trees, about two hundred yards away.

"I feel . . . so . . . floppy," Piper huffed, breathing heavily as she lurched down the beach.

"Just . . . keep . . . going," Prue managed to say before she tripped on a shell and tumbled to the sand. Piper stopped and turned back to help Prue to her feet. As she did, she heard the Sirens' horrible screams echo over the beach.

"The time freeze," Prue said, feeling stronger with each passing second. "It's ended. How do you feel, Piper?"

"A little stronger," Piper said, shaking her head hard.

"Me, too," Prue said. "I think we can outrun them."

The sisters turned and began to gallop toward the trees. They were halfway there when Piper felt something whiz by her face. She gasped as she saw the lead Siren's sharp blade crash into the sand before her. It must have missed her by only a centimeter!

Gasping for breath, Piper whirled around. The brown-haired bird-woman stood on the beach about twenty feet away, screaming in rage. Her two flunkies stood at her side. Their lyre and flute had disappeared, and in their place were knives of their own. Siren #2 passed her weapon to the leader. The hideous bird-woman clutched the blade and reared back. She was going to throw the knife!

Before she could think twice, Piper reached for the waistband of her leggings. Her fingers closed around the silver letter opener she'd brought for Charon. She hauled back and flung the blade at the lead Siren. Then she gasped in surprise as she saw the knife make a direct hit, piercing the creature's heart. Green blood oozed from the wound, spilling out over her white feathers. With another scream of rage, the Siren fell to the sand. The other bird-women emitted horrible screeches and threw their wings around their leader, wailing and moaning. That's when Piper froze time again.

"Let's get out of here before they take revenge," she shouted at Prue. By now the sisters felt strong enough to sprint the rest of the way to the trees. In a few moments, they'd plunged into the forest. They began hiking quickly through the woods, leaping over fallen logs and sloshing through shallow streams.

"I don't think they're following us," Piper huffed. "They probably can't fly through the thick foliage."

"Even so," Prue called back as she crashed through a glade of ferns. "I want to put as much distance between us and those Sirens as possible. I can't believe what power their song had over us."

"The myths say only the most heroic sailors could survive their attack," Piper said, using some stepping stones to cross a stream. "Thank goodness we were able to escape them!"

"I guess it just takes a witch's touch," Prue said, grinning as she hurried down a muddy path.

The sisters pressed on, hiking for another mile or so before Prue stopped suddenly.

"Piper!" she yelled.

Piper, who'd been walking determinedly, her head down, looked back at her sister.

"Look around us!" Prue exclaimed. "I think we're back on Nikos's turf!"

Piper gazed around and gasped. Without their even noticing, the terrain had gone from lush and green to brown and swampy. The fresh smell of the jungle had been replaced by the dank funk of the marsh. The trees had lost their leaves and their trunks had withered.

"Look for the mountain," Piper said suddenly. "Remember, the cave was at the base of a really tall, craggy mountain. More like a pile of boulders, actually."

The sisters gazed up, straining to see through the trees.

"There!" Prue cried, pointing to their left. Through a mist they could faintly see a looming, craggy shape. "That has to be it."

"And look!" Piper screamed, pointing at the ground nearby. "The stream that led us to the cave last time!"

"Phoebe, here we come!" Prue yelled. With that, she and Piper took off through the woods.

Phoebe slumped in her gilded chair in the enormous dining room and tried to keep her eyes open. The banquet had dragged on for hours, yet the guests never seemed to tire. They slugged back glass after glass of wine, devoured course after course of rich food, laughed a million times at meaningless repartee.

Jessica hadn't been kidding when she'd said life in Hades was one long party. That's *all* it was—and it was unspeakably empty. The party guests, all of whom had the same glossy black curls and the same cold, vacant eyes as Nikos and Jessica, had tried to engage her in conversation for about a minute. When Phoebe clamped her mouth shut, refusing to speak and staring at them sullenly, they shrugged and turned away. After that, it was as if she didn't exist. They gazed through her and spoke over her head.

"Strike two with the in-laws," Phoebe had muttered, rolling her eyes.

She glanced at the man at the head of the table, who had to be Hades, god of the underworld. Phoebe saw Nikos's dark blue eyes and strong jaw in the man. His curls were pitch-black, too, but for a few sparkling strands of silver. He was large and imposing, but other than that, Phoebe was shocked that he was such a powerful god. He looked as shallow as everyone else at the banquet, too immersed in his own enjoyment to even glance at his prospective daughter-in-law. He merely laughed, slugged back wine, and flirted with snake maidens. Phoebe rolled her eyes and looked away.

In fact, for about the millionth time, her eyes drifted to the groaning plate in front of her. Beef tenderloin and potatoes drowning in butter seemed to taunt her. Crusty rolls beckoned from her bread plate. A cornucopia of fruit spilled onto the tablecloth in front of her, and a glass of fragrant red wine sat at her elbow.

Phoebe sighed and glared at Nikos, who sat several seats away from her. She was so tired and so hungry. She didn't know how she was going to make it through the rest of this night.

Simply to occupy her hands, she plucked a pomegranate out of the cornucopia and began rolling it around in her palm. She'd loved pomegranates when she was little. Grams had always had them around at Thanksgiving. Phoebe loved peeling the tough, berry-colored skin away to reveal the clusters of shiny seeds. Every seed exploded with tart, sweet juice when you bit down on it. And they stained your lips bright red, which had thrilled Phoebe to no end in her prelipstick years.

Listlessly, almost without being aware of it, Phoebe began peeling away this pomegranate's skin. She pulled at the white membrane underneath to reveal a pod of plump pomegranate seeds.

They're so pretty, she mused. They look like rubies. Just like the triangular rubies on her engagement ring, as a matter of fact.

Phoebe emitted a small, almost silent sob. The hated ring was fused to her hand. She might as well face it. She was going to spend the rest of her life in this cold, horrible place with these sickening, vapid people. There was no hope. And there was no way she could escape, not when she was so drained of energy, so very, very hungry.

As if in a trance, Phoebe began to pluck the pomegranate seeds out of the fruit, scattering them on the white tablecloth. She gazed at them. They looked so alluring, so succulent. She picked one up and stared at it. Then slowly, she began to bring it to her lips.

"Phoebe! No!"

Phoebe gasped and looked up. Where had that voice come from? She looked quickly around but nobody at the table was looking at her. They continued to chatter among themselves, swilling more and more wine, gnawing at meaty bones, and slurping big spoonfuls of soup. Was she hallucinating from hunger?

"Behind you!"

Phoebe froze. Then slowly, she turned in her chair. Piper was crouched on the floor, hiding behind the imposing wooden back of Phoebe's chair.

"Piper," Phoebe squealed softly, reaching down to clutch at her sister's hands. Tears sprang to her eyes. "Oh, I never thought I'd see you again."

"Have you eaten anything since you've been here?" Piper asked urgently.

"Ugh, no," Phoebe said, surprised. "I went on a hunger strike. Why?"

"That's fabulous news," Piper whispered, grinning at her sister through tears of her own. "Okay, we're going to get you out of here. Prue's behind the door."

Piper nodded at the dining room entrance.

"We've been peeking in," she continued. "Everybody seems to be oblivious to you. It's really weird."

"I think it's because I haven't eaten the food," Phoebe replied. "I think the grub is enchanted or something. It turns everyone into an empty-headed party animal. I so don't fit in. Ironic, isn't it?"

"The girl who knows every dance club in San

Francisco," Piper agreed with a grin. "Anyway, if you get up and walk out, very slowly and calmly, I think they might not notice. Nobody even glanced in my direction when I crawled in."

"Okay," Phoebe said as Piper slunk away. Phoebe turned slowly and gazed around. Nothing had changed—the air was still thick with conversation and boozy laughter. Several seats down the table, Nikos was clinking glasses with a snake maiden and nibbling her earlobe.

Yuck, Phoebe thought. I guess he wants to live up his last moments as a bachelor. Be my guest. Now's my chance.

Slowly, Phoebe pushed back her chair and slid off her seat. Then she lifted her long skirts and crouched to the floor. Silently, she slunk through the long dining room until finally, she reached the door. With one more stealthy glance backward, she slipped out of the room, falling into Prue's waiting arms.

"Oh, Prue," she wept, "it's awful. Nikos is trying to force me to marry him. His father has decreed that if he isn't married by August fifteenth, he'll be banished to earth and all his powers will die."

"What's August fifteenth?" Prue asked, stroking Phoebe's brittle curls soothingly.

"His twenty-fifth birthday," Phoebe explained. "We've got to get away, now. The wedding's supposed to be in the morning!"

"You're gonna be okay, Phoebs," Prue whispered, hugging her sister hard. "We'll be out of here soon. But first, do you know where Nikos is keeping the models?"

Phoebe nodded.

"In the dungeon," she said. "I hope you can break through the door with your powers."

"Let's go," Prue said. "Lead the way."

The sisters were heading out of the foyer when suddenly, a figure shimmered into their path, blocking the way. Nikos! He was still holding his wine glass. He must have shimmered out of the banquet the moment he noticed Phoebe's absence.

The spoiled prince snarled at his fiancée.

"I warned you, Phoebe," he screamed, throwing his glass to the floor, where it shattered. Then he lifted his hand and swung at Phoebe's face. An instant before his knuckles connected with her cheekbone, his hand was thrown backward, as if it had bounced off a rubber wall.

Nikos gaped in confusion. Then he swiped at Phoebe again. His hand bounced away again.

"What?" he blurted.

"That's Zeus's doing," Piper announced, grabbing Phoebe's shoulders. "He's decreed that Phoebe is free. She's under his protection. We all are. We're taking her home."

"What . . . no . . . that can't be!" Nikos bellowed.

"It is," Prue spat. "So deal with it."

Nikos screamed with rage, his glowing red eyes bulging out of his dark face. Then, abruptly, he grew quiet. And an evil smile began to play across his lips.

"All right, so you've got her," he said, crossing his arms across his chest in defiance. "But *I* have your beautiful friends. Five innocents—innocents who will die, one by one, until Phoebe agrees to marry me."

CHAPTER 13

As Nikos uttered his threat, he clapped his hands over his head. Instantly, three snake servants slithered out and bowed before the prince.

"Get the prisoners," Nikos ordered. "Now!"

The servants shimmered out of the room. They returned almost immediately, carrying the five models in their arms. Even though it was just their souls that were trapped in Hades, the models looked physically haggard. Chloe's sharp cheekbones were even more sunken than usual, and Kurt's muscular arms were limp and weak. They were disheveled and dirt-smeared and shivering in their torn, limp Grecian costumes. The models clung to each other and stared at Nikos fearfully. When Chloe saw Prue, Piper, and Phoebe, she cried out.

"Where have you been?" she wailed.

Nikos stalked over to Chloe and slung his arm

around her waist. He ripped her from the group and
dragged her into the center of the floor.

"You know, Chloe, I don't like you," he taunted.
"You complain too much."

With that, he whipped a knife out of his velvet suit
and pressed it against Chloe's long, slender throat.

"Aaaaiiigh," she screamed, gasping for breath.

Involuntarily, Piper waved her hands at Nikos,
forgetting that her freezing power was useless on
him. Prue dropped into fighting stance, getting ready
to pounce at Nikos's slightest move. But then the
prince lifted his blade from the model's neck. He
tossed her aside and sheathed his knife.

"No, I won't kill her myself," he said blandly.
"That sort of labor is beneath a prince. I have min-
ions for that."

Nikos snapped his fingers, and a figure shimmered into the foyer. A lurching, slope-shouldered
beast with crusty green skin and a long, razor-
sharp tail.

"Mitchell!" Prue spat.

"Mitchell?" Piper and Phoebe blurted together.
They gaped at the lumbering, unspeakably ugly
demon.

"But," Piper stuttered, "but you were—"

"My lord of the underworld but you girls are
dense, aren't you?" Nikos burst out. "One look at a
'hottie' and you lose it completely. You couldn't tell a
demon from Matt Damon!"

"Hey!" Mitchell growled, curling his blackened
lips and drooling angrily. "You could give me a little
credit for deceiving them."

"No offense," Nikos said, rolling his eyes. He

stalked to the wall and leaned against it, crossing his ankles lazily. Then he gave Mitchell a little wave.

"All right," he said, "Hop to. Kill the blond one. *Unless* Phoebe agrees to our terms."

"No!" Phoebe screamed. "Leave her alone!"

"Then marry me," Nikos ordered.

Phoebe gasped, looking wildly from Nikos to Chloe to her sisters. What should she do? Save the innocent's life and destroy the Power of Three in the process? That would put the lives of the people who needed them in the future at risk. Should she sacrifice Chloe so she could go back to earth? No! She couldn't do that! Her head was spinning.

"Prue, Piper," she whispered weakly. "Help me!"

Prue watched Mitchell approach Chloe, who was crouching and squealing with fear. Prue had to do something. But what?

She glanced at Nikos, still smirking on the sidelines. Then it came to her.

"Hey!" she shouted at Mitchell. The demon turned away from Chloe and glared at her.

"You're so easily offended," she taunted. "Well, how about this, Mitchell? You're pathetic as a demon! You could barely hit me."

She turned to her sisters.

"I vanquished this loser with his own tail," she said. "Isn't that hilarious?"

Prue burst into maniacal laughter. Nervously, Piper and Phoebe joined in with tepid giggles.

"What is she doing?" Phoebe whispered through gritted teeth.

"Don't know," Piper muttered back. "Just go with it."

Mitchell, for one, was not laughing. He just curled a lip at Prue and took another plodding step toward Chloe.

"And you know, you're not really that great a kisser," Prue continued quickly. "If you hadn't put a spell on those smooches, I would have been yawning my way through those dates."

Mitchell spun around, flinging a wad of drool as he did. He glowered at Prue.

"Oh, right," he grunted, rolling his yellow eyes. "Forget that. You were so whipped."

"Ha!" Prue barked. "How could I fall for such a rotten journalist? Your prose is awkward, and your reporting skills suck!"

With that, Mitchell forgot Chloe. He threw back his head and roared. Then he spun around and rushed at Prue, digging his claws into her arms and breathing hotly into her face, just as he had at Halliwell Manor.

"You don't know what you're talking about," he huffed.

"Oh, I think I know exactly what I'm talking about," Prue retorted. "You sold your soul to the prince of Hades. In exchange for being his big dumb lunk of a minion, your mortal self got a slot at *National Geographic*, the pinnacle of your profession."

Mitchell screamed, his eyes glowing red. At that moment Prue knew that her hunch was correct. Mitchell may have sold his soul, but clearly he still had his pride. His work was his Achilles' heel.

"I know why that bothers you so much," Prue said. "Because you're a hack. You could never get by on talent. Without Nikos, you'd be nothing."

Mitchell hauled back and punched Prue across the jaw.

"Prue!" Piper and Phoebe screamed, jumping to assist her. But Prue thrust her hand out, holding them back.

"This is my fight," she muttered, rubbing her jaw.

"Oh, isn't that typical," Mitchell growled sarcastically. "Little Miss Perfect Prue! Always together. Always in control. Everything's so easy for you."

"Jealous?" Prue said.

Mitchell socked her again. Prue was so incensed she barely felt the harsh blow.

"Oh, please," she taunted. "Is that your best shot?"

With that, Mitchell started swinging wildly at Prue. Channeling her rage into expert fighting skills, she ducked his punches and blocked his swings, countering with killer blows of her own. She swung brutal kicks to Mitchell's side, legs, and gut.

In a few minutes, she had him tired out.

That's when she pulled out the big guns.

"Freeze him," she yelled at Piper. Immediately, Piper complied, waving her hands at Mitchell and freezing him in midpunch.

While he hovered, helpless, in midair, Prue used her telekinesis to throw him against the stone wall. The force of the impact unfroze him and he shook his head, looking around woozily.

"How did I get here?" he growled.

"Again!" Prue ordered.

Piper shot another freeze at Mitchell, and Prue crashed him into the wall once more. Two more times she repeated the vicious cycle. Each time, Mitchell staggered to his feet, looking more bleary and weary with the blows.

"Again!" Prue shouted.

Piper began to wave her hands.

"No!" Mitchell cried, holding out one of his enormous claws. "Stop. Please. I can't take any more."

"What?"

That was Nikos, who'd been watching the entire scene with amusement. Now, however, he was incensed.

"You are my demon!" Nikos bellowed. "You will do as ordered. Now kill the girl."

"Piper . . ." Prue said.

"No!" Mitchell screamed. "Don't freeze me again. I can't . . . I can't."

He slumped to the floor in a quivering heap, burying his scaly head in his claws.

"Defeated by women?" Nikos yelled. "Worthless creature!"

"You could have jumped in to help me," Mitchell accused, rolling his yellow eyes to gaze at Nikos balefully.

"As I said, hand-to-hand combat is beneath me. That's a demon's job," Nikos snapped. "Besides, I wanted to see what you were made of. Now that I know, I have no use for you."

"What?" Mitchell cried. "But we had a deal!"

Mitchell crawled to Nikos's feet, clutching his knees, weeping in panic.

"Please, please don't kill me!" he sobbed. "We had a deeeaaal."

"Oh, please," Nikos muttered in disgust. "Your

miserable life is safe with me. Our deal, however, is off."

Mitchell gaped at Nikos as the prince waved one finger at him. With that, the demon was transformed back into his human self. But any cuteness he'd had was destroyed by his quivering expression, his heaving, submissive posture, and the loathsome, selfish stare in his eyes.

"I . . . I don't understand," Mitchell said.

"I'm releasing you from your service to Hades," Nikos snapped impatiently. "You will go back to earth as a human. Mortal. Boooring."

"But," Mitchell sputtered, "my career!"

"Take it up with human resources!" Nikos bellowed. "I'm so over you."

With that, he flicked his finger at Mitchell. The quivering young man screamed as he was transformed into a whoosh of shimmering light. The light shot from the room, out of the palace, and back to earth.

Shaking his head in disgust, Nikos pulled his knife back out of its sheath.

"I suppose I'll have to do this myself," he complained. "It's impossible to find good help these days!"

He stomped over to Chloe and grabbed her again. Cruelly, he waved the knife in front of Chloe's nose, giggling as she shrieked in terror.

"Phoebe," the beautiful young woman squeaked, "Please . . ."

"Yes, Phoebe," Nikos said. "It's come down to the wire. What'll it be? Your hand . . . or Chloe's life?"

Tearfully, Phoebe opened her mouth to answer.

She couldn't let an innocent person die for her. She had to submit to Nikos.

Giving her sisters an anguished glance, she trudged toward Nikos. She swallowed hard and began to speak.

"The bond which was not to be done, give us the power to see it undone!"

It was Prue—shouting some lines of verse across the foyer. Phoebe and Nikos both whirled around to stare at her.

"What is that?" Nikos sneered. "A farewell poem?"

"In a manner of speaking," Prue shot back as she fished a crumpled scrap of paper out of her shorts pocket. " 'The bond which was not to be done, give us the power to see it undone. And move time forward, for thee we shun!' "

Phoebe shook her head in confusion. That poem, it sounded so familiar. Then she gasped. That's no poem, she thought, that's my time-travel spell. But why?

Piper gaped at Prue. Halfway through her sister's recital, she recognized the verse as a spell. I think that's Phoebe's time-travel spell, she thought. But . . . why?

As she recited Phoebe's words, Prue gazed urgently into her sisters' eyes. Trust me, she willed them. Trust me. Say it with me.

Prue began to recite the spell a second time. With confusion still in her brown eyes, Phoebe nevertheless joined in, her voice strong and clear. Immediately, Piper began to say the words with them.

"What are you doing?" Nikos screamed, hurling

Chloe out of his way and stomping over to Prue. "Whatever it is, I suggest you stop. You'll be very, very sorry if you cross me."

Prue heard Nikos's threats, but she closed her eyes and ignored them. Must finish the incantation, she thought as she and her sisters launched into the spell a third time.

"That's it," Nikos screamed. He stalked back over to Chloe.

" 'Give us the power to see it undone'," the sisters recited desperately.

"I'm going to kill her now!" Nikos shouted.

" 'And move time forward,' " the witches shrieked.

Nikos raised his blade.

" 'For thee we shun!' " They'd finished the incantation.

Instantly, a wind whipped through the foyer, knocking the mortals to the ground and whipping the blade from Nikos's hand.

"Aiiiigh!" he screamed in rage. He spotted the knife on the floor. He wiggled his finger at it to shimmer the weapon back into his hands.

The blade sat on the floor. It didn't move an inch.

"What?" Nikos blurted. Then he stood straight and closed his eyes. Phoebe recognized his projection stance. He was trying to shimmer from one place to another.

But nothing happened.

"My . . . my powers," Nikos cried. "I don't under—"

"My, my, look at the time," Prue said smugly, gazing at her watch. "I've got August fifteenth."

"My birthday!" Nikos said, looking stunned.

"Time-travel spell," Phoebe explained. "An old Halliwell favorite. We've just jumped ahead two days."

"No!" Nikos cried, flailing his arms wildly, trying to work his magic. "It's not possible."

"Sorry, it's already done," Phoebe said with mock sympathy. "And what was it you told me? I believe your exact words were, 'My father's spell has already been cast. If there's not a ring on my finger the morning of my twenty-fifth birthday, I'll instantly be sent . . . up there. Doomed to live a humdrum life with no power, no magic, walking among mortals.' "

Nikos fell to his knees, utterly stupefied. He trembled with fear and disbelief.

"No," he rasped. "No, it can't be."

"Uh, Nikos," Prue said, stepping forward. "Take it up with human resources. See you on earth!"

With that, she flicked her finger, Nikos style, at the quivering prince. He began to fly through the air, howling. Halfway across the room, his body shimmered away and he was transformed into a streak of light, just as Mitchell had been. An instant later the light shot from the room. Nikos had been banished.

Phoebe glanced at the dining room door.

"Wow," she said. "Those people have been partying for four days and they're still going strong. Let's get out of here before they notice that Nikos has disappeared."

Grabbing the hands of the trembling models, the witches led the way out of the palace into the gloom of Hades.

As they began the long hike through the woods,

Prue said, "I propose we exit through the 'front door.' I'd much rather face Charon again than those dreadful Sirens. Plus, we still have something for our fare."

She reached into her pocket and pulled out the beautiful mother-of-pearl inkwell.

"Our only problem is the models," Piper whispered, glancing at the delicate, wispy beauties, who were already stumbling and stubbing their toes on the rough path. "Think they can hack it?"

"Oh, believe me," Phoebe said, "They can make it. The real question is, can we survive their complaining."

"I mean really," Chloe was saying. "Two days we were stuck there and not one magazine? And the bathrooms were totally primitive!"

"Ugh," Prue said with a laugh. "Let's get going. This is going to be the hike from hell."

"But at least we're doing it together," Phoebe said, smiling gratefully at her sisters. "We've got our Power of Three back. That's all the strength I need!"

CHAPTER

14

Anybody home?" Prue called, slamming the front door and racing into the foyer. She crossed the living room, glancing into the empty—blissfully empty—sunroom. Then she stepped around the stone Gorgon and headed into the kitchen.

She found Piper and Phoebe sitting at their new kitchen table. Piper was sipping a glass of iced tea, and Phoebe was assembling an enormous sandwich out of a small mountain of deli meats, cheeses, and condiments. Prue had to laugh.

"What?" Phoebe protested, flipping a strand of blond hair out of her eyes. "It's my after-school snack. You know I'm always starving after my painting class."

"I hope it's not some cute guy that's got your metabolism going," Prue said, striding across the room and flopping into a chair between her sisters.

"No way!" Phoebe said, taking an enormous bite

from her sandwich. "The only guy I'm involved with at the moment is Vincent van Gogh."

Prue smiled and shook her head.

"It's hard to believe that only a week ago we were slogging through Hades."

"With five fashion models!" Piper blurted, giggling.

"Thank goodness they didn't remember a thing when they woke up in the sunroom," Phoebe pointed out as she popped an olive into her mouth.

"Yeah," Prue said. "And all it took was one more handy-dandy time-travel spell to erase the fact that they'd just taken a two-day nap."

"That was a lot easier than getting my old blond 'do back," Phoebe added. "I spent like three hours at the salon undoing Nikos's damage! My hairdresser thought I had gone nuts."

She twirled a tendril of silky blond hair around her finger and grinned while Prue and Piper laughed out loud.

"So, anyway," Piper said, turning to Prue, "what are you so excited about that you, Prue Halliwell, slammed the front door, à la Phoebe?"

"Hey," Phoebe protested, throwing a corn chip at Piper.

"I was just at *415*," Prue announced, pulling her gorgeous faux-Victorian print out of her portfolio to show her sisters. "Mr. Caldwell loved the photo! He called it 'magical.' "

"Insightful guy, your editor," Phoebe said dryly.

"And I got the cover!" Prue said.

"Prue, that's fabulous," Piper shrieked.

"You are so kicking butt," Phoebe agreed. "And

you didn't have to sell your soul to do it! Pure talent—that's my sis."

"Which reminds me of the other thing I saw today," Prue said. She grinned and pulled a thin newspaper out of her bag. "Check this out."

She flipped through the tabloid size newspaper—one of the less-distinguished free weeklies scattered around San Francisco—and came to one of the last pages.

"It's an obituary," Phoebe said, looking at Prue blankly. "Do we know this person? And why are you looking so amused, Prue? The man's dead. And he was only ninety-seven!"

"Not the subject," Prue said. "The author. Look at the byline."

"Obituary by staff writer Mitchell Pearl," Piper read. Then her eyes widened. "Mitchell? Your Mitchell?"

"Yup!" Prue giggled. "Without Nikos's evil influence, I guess the only gig he could get was an entry-level job at a fish-wrapper."

The sisters burst into laughter.

"And what about the newly mortal Nikos?" Piper said to Phoebe. "Seen him around town?"

Phoebe shook her head.

"Maybe I should check the reptile house at the zoo," she sneered. "I know he's partial to snakes."

"So, I think this is a record," Prue said dryly, grabbing one of Phoebe's chips. "Two of us fell for demons at the same time."

"Ugh, I know!" Phoebe said. "Why, oh why do we have such bad luck with men?"

"Well, at least Prue got some necking out of it," Piper teased, poking her in the arm.

"Hey," Prue protested. "You promised you wouldn't mention it again if I did your laundry for the next month."

"Mention what?" Piper teased. "That you almost abandoned me on Mount Olympus because you were making out with a guy?"

"Aaaaigh!" Prue shrieked with a laugh. "You promised!"

"That's the last you'll hear of it," Piper said, getting up to fix Prue some iced tea. "Witch's honor."

Phoebe took a bite of a pickle and chewed thoughtfully for a moment.

"We should look at the bright side," she announced. "Maybe we'll meet some hot new guys, *nondemon*, thank you very much, when we go to Heaven tonight."

"What?" Prue and Piper blurted.

"Didn't we just put all that stuff behind us?" Piper demanded, sitting back down at the table with Prue's tea.

"Not Mount Olympus," Phoebe said. "Heaven—the cabaret! We vowed that when Prue made her deadline, we would paint the town red. You were angsting about your life being too boring, Piper. Remember?"

"Please," Piper said with another laugh. "I've been to Mount Olympus. I've vanquished a three-headed dog, a Gorgon, and some Sirens. I've been to Hades and back. My life is anything but boring."

Phoebe took another huge bite out of her sandwich and grinned at her sisters. "I'll eat to that!"

"You know, we have one bit of unfinished business after this whole Hades mess," Piper reminded them.

Prue nodded. Then all three sisters twisted in their seats to glare at the Gorgon in the kitchen doorway. It was the ugliest sculpture imaginable and totally in the way. All week, they'd been trying to figure out how to get the thing—which must have weighed a thousand pounds—out of their house. They couldn't call in a professional mover, they'd agreed—it would look too suspicious. And, even with a dolly, they wouldn't have been able to get it down the steps without doing major damage.

"Well, funny you should mention our Gorgon friend, Piper," Phoebe said. She grinned sneakily and headed to the broom closet on the other side of the kitchen. "Because I think I came up with a solution today. I made a little trip to the hardware store and bought . . . these!"

Phoebe spun around and held up three sledge-hammers.

"Phoebe," Piper said, slapping her forehead. "Of course. You're brilliant!"

"So, you ready to play whack-a-Gorgon?" Phoebe said.

"Oh yeah," Prue declared. "Let me at it."

The sisters each grasped a hammer. Then they circled the Gorgon.

"Who gets the first crack?" Piper asked.

"I think Phoebe should," Prue said. "After all, she was the one held hostage."

"And don't forget the hair," Piper pointed out with a giggle.

Phoebe grinned at her sisters. Then she swung her sledgehammer over her head.

"Hiiiii-YAH!" she screamed, bringing it down on

the stone Gorgon with a clang. A cluster of snakes crumbled and snapped off the statue's head.

"Yah!" Piper yelled, joining in. She whacked the Gorgon's hand off. Then Prue went to work, smashing at the statue's feet. The sisters laughed as they destroyed the creature who'd almost done them in.

In a few minutes they were breathing heavily, and the Gorgon had been reduced to a pile of rubble at their feet.

"I'll get some garbage bags," Phoebe volunteered.

"I'll get the broom," Piper said, skipping across the kitchen.

"And I'll just make a general declaration to anyone who might be listening," Prue said. She pointed at the floor. "And this means you! Don't mess with the Charmed Ones!"

About the Author

ELIZABETH LENHARD is the author of Pocket Books' *Clueless*®: *Bettypalooza* and the novelizations *Charlie's Angels* and *Dudley Do-Right*. She has also written horror and sci-fi thrillers for young readers. A former staff writer for the *Atlanta Journal-Constitution*, she is now a contributing dining critic at *Chicago* magazine and a columnist at *Swoon*. She lives and writes in the shadow of Wrigley Field, in Chicago.

BEWARE WHAT YOU WISH

Wishes are being made all over San Francisco: a candidate for office wishes for a less formidable opponent, a little girl wishes for a horse, and Phoebe wishes she could foresee more calamities so she can prevent them. Soon she's having more visions than she can handle – and the sisters are exhausted from racing all over town to avert disasters. Finally Phoebe refuses even to leave the house!

A strange spirit has been released from its stone prison, and the power of the Charmed Ones may not be enough to stop an impending cataclysm . . .

F E A R L E S S

. . . a girl born without the fear gene

Seventeen-year-old Gaia Moore is not your typical high school senior. She is a black belt in karate, was doing advanced maths in junior school and, oh yes, she absolutely Does Not Care. About anything. Her mother is dead and her father, a covert anti-terrorist agent, abandoned her years ago. But before he did, he taught her self-preservation. Tom Moore knew there would be a lot of people after Gaia because of who, and what, she is. Gaia is genetically enhanced not to feel fear and her life has suddenly become dangerous. Her world is about to explode with terrorists, government spies and psychos bent on taking her apart. But Gaia does not care. She is Fearless.

Read Francine Pascal's gripping new series
Available now from Pocket Books

Some secrets are too dangerous to know . . .

ROSWELL
HIGH

In the tiny town of Roswell, New Mexico, teenagers Liz Parker and Max Evans forged an otherworldly connection after Max recklessly threw aside his pact of secrecy and healed a life-threatening wound of Liz's with the touch of his hand. It turns out that Max, his sister Isabel, and their friend Michael are surviving descendants from beings on board an alien spacecraft which crash-landed in Roswell in 1947.

Max loves Liz. He couldn't let her die. But this is a dangerous secret he swore never to divulge - and now it's out. The trio must learn to trust Liz and her best friend Maria in order to stay one step ahead of the sheriff and the FBI who will stop at nothing in hunting out an alien…